IDA MAE TUTWEILER AND THE TRAVELING TEA PARTY

By
Ginnie Siena Bivona

To Donna...
With warmest regards!
Ginnie Siena Bivona

authorlink press
www.authorlink.com

Published by Authorlink Press
An imprint of Authorlink
(http://www.authorlink.com)
3720 Millswood Dr.
Irving, Texas 75062, USA

First published by Authorlink Press
An imprint of Authorlink
First Printing, March, 2000

Printed in the United States of America

ISBN 1 928704 15 8

Dedicated to the DFW Writers Workshop

Without their loving support, encouragement,
and weekly flayings (euphemistically titled "critique"),
this book would never have happened.
To some special few I owe more than just a simple thanks.
I dare to call myself a writer because of them.

Author's Notes

This is a work of fiction. All the names, characters, organizations, and events portrayed in this book are either the product of the author's imagination or are used fictitiously for verisimilitude. Any other resemblance to any organization, event, or actual person, living or dead, is unintended and entirely coincidental.

Acknowledgements

This book came from my heart. I don't know how long it was there before I put it on paper, but it must have been a while, because it spilled out onto the pages so fast. (The first time. The re-write almost became a lifetime hobby.)

I know the joy of long-time friendships. My life is full and beautiful because of my beloved friends.

Some of this book is almost true; the rest is made up out of the whole cloth. And a few things are absolutely true. My mother died of breast cancer when I was 24. I know how it feels to lose a mother too young. I also know that Jane's death from breast cancer denied is based on truth.

While writing this book I sought medical opinion and was told of a woman, currently in the last stages of cancer, who actually went for a *year and a half* with a lump in her breast, until a friend took her, almost by force, to the doctor.

How could anyone, in this day and age, with so much information all around us, ignore or deny the obvious signs and symptoms of breast cancer? I don't pretend to know the answer to that tragic question, but I can only hope that perhaps one woman will read this book, recognize herself, and go for medical attention.

Before the door closes.

My deepest thanks to my editor, Doris Booth. The woman is a marvel.

Also, fervent thanks to Susan K. Malone. Without her fine editing and wise advice the book would never have made it past the first wastebasket. May blessings be heaped on the head of Beth Kohler, who line edited, and line edited, and *line edited* the manuscript.

Thanks to Alan Kaye, MD, who took time to explain to me what I could and could not do medically. And to my dear

Susan Acosta, RN, treasured friend and nurse advisor. Special thanks to my favorite boss, Dianne Stultz, for her support and understanding.

And of course, I thank my children. All five of them. Without them, I am nothing. My darling daughters, Stephanie and Elizabeth; their encouragement gives me the energy and desire to go on when what I'd really like to do is skip it all and take a nice long nap. Mark, my talented eldest son; his artistic photography graces this cover. He can't even begin to imagine what a joy it is to work with my own son on something as important in my life as this book is to me. Maybe someday he'll be as lucky as I am. And then there's Matt, my youngest, and Larry, the second oldest; two of the finest young men on the continent. The love of these wonderful young people is, indeed, "the wind beneath *my* wings."

Chapter One

To my way of thinking there's simply nothing that smoothes away the sharp edges of the day quite like a nice hot cup of tea, served late in the afternoon, with a bit of a cookie or a scone alongside. Scones are best, of course, if you can find the time to make them. Jane will be here in a few minutes. Dear old anything-but-plain Jane. She's the only woman I've ever known who can hold her own with the boys and knows exactly how to hold a cup like a lady.

The table is set in the sunroom. It's my favorite place in this huge old house. Never mind that the wicker chairs are a hundred years rickety, and only a few scattered chips of the original bright yellow paint remain. Never mind that the plants have a dusty, unkempt look (I don't claim to have a green thumb). Even on the drabbest days there's something comforting about being in here.

Mum's teapot (yes, I still have it after all these years) sits patiently waiting on the sink beside the stove. It's already been filled with hot water to warm it up. The little silver tea ball filled with Earl Grey rests beside it, ready to pop inside its elderly rounded belly. I won't turn the kettle on until she gets here.

Anyone who knows anything about tea knows you must get the water just to a full boil. You can't make proper tea till everyone is at the table. I've gotten the water hot, though; it won't take but a minute to get it right.

The doorbell rings; the sound jars in the tiled kitchen. I quickly turn on the fire under the kettle before I go to let her in.

On my tenth birthday Mum gave me my first diary. She wrapped it in white tissue and tied a red ribbon around it.

"This is your secrets book," she said to me. "You can write anything you want in here, and it's only for you to see. Not even I can read it." She showed me the clever little lock and tiny key that sealed it from all other's eyes. I was surprised at Mum giving me such a strange and wonderful gift.

"Do you have one?" I asked.

"That's for me to know, not you." She winked at me, and I remember how delicious her laughter sounded. Almost as delicious as the sweet milky tea and Aunt Germaine's prize-winning orange marmalade-filled scones we shared in celebration of the day.

The first entry: May 15, 1935, (written in a careful round hand, all the i's dotted with tiny circles.)

Dear Diary,

I don't know what I'll write in here, but Mum says this is my very own secret place and I'm to write down whatever I want. Nobody, not even Mum, can read it.

Today was my birthday and Mum gave me this book. Aunt Germaine gave me a new green scarf to go with my winter coat. Why would she give me something I can't even wear till winter? I don't think she much likes me.

They couldn't come to tea for my birthday because Bernadette was sick again. She is forever getting sick. I don't like her even if she is my cousin. So there. Here's my first secret. I DON'T LIKE MY FAT COUSIN BERNADETTE. Aunt Germaine is always comparing her to me, and she is smarter, prettier, and better at everything in the whole wide world than I am.

She is mean to me and sneaky too, and she never gets caught. I'm the one who always gets in all the trouble.

Signed, Ida Mae Hampton.

Jane bursts through the door.

Now that I think of it, I don't recall ever seeing Jane simply walk in anywhere. Off stage or on, she makes an entrance, into the house or into a room. I wonder what she looks like early in the morning going to the bathroom.

"Darling, darling, darling, happy birthday to you!" she trills. Packages are flung at me, and she whirls to grab still another bag left outside the door. It matters not to her that my birthday was months ago. Whenever she brings gifts, it's my birthday.

Jane is not the least bit beautiful, and yet when you first see her, you think she is. Later you'll say she is stunning or striking, but not beautiful. It's the elegantly coifed masses of jet black hair, the greenest eyes the contact lens people could create, a bit of clever surgery, and a figure that she straps and wraps and cajoles into a junoesque centerfold marvel.

She smells like a French whore. But a very rich French whore, I must admit. I love her as much as anyone in my life. She is the life in my life.

August 18, 1939

Dear Diary,

Today I made a new friend. I think. She is very nice. Her name is Jane Potter. She is in my grade and we sit beside each other in math and homeroom. She is lots taller than me and braver, too. She is not afraid to talk to anyone, even the boys. I could never do that. I feel dumb. It's hard for me to talk to the girls, and I really can't think of a thing to say to a boy. I'm always afraid they will not like me or something. I wish I knew how to be better but I don't.

Jane is just very outgoing. That's what Mr. Goodwin said in math class. He told her she was very outgoing but that she was going to have to let him run the class. She told him he could unless she thought he was doing something wrong, then she'd have to step in. The whole class laughed and even Mr. Goodwin smiled.

I don't know why she bothers with me but she does and I'm glad.

Signed, Ida Mae Hampton.

Jane grew up in the rich part of town. Well, rich for Walton Falls. She was an only child, like me, and lived in a huge brick house out on Old Mill Road. Being brick automatically made it a mansion. A notion that made Jane laugh wildly.

The house had a huge back yard, terraced down to a clear, fast-running creek. We loved playing down there; it was cool when the rest of Ohio was stifling in the summer heat. Her mother always reminded us not to play in that dirty creek water. We did anyway. We just made sure we dried out before we went back to the house.

We loved grubbing around in the woods, hunting down old discarded stained-glass windows. We had a great collection of the round faceted stones that had been set in the designs. Christmas red and sapphire blue, golden amber and clear glass, they sparkled like rare jewels in the sunlight.

Nowadays, of course, no one would dream of throwing out a wonderful stained-glass window, but in those days they were considered hopelessly out of date. Anyone who could afford it had them removed and replaced with the much more fashionable window glass.

That suited me and Jane to a T. We spent hours hunting down those abandoned treasures. And talking, talking, always talking. We talked about everything except the things that caused us the most concern, and those were never mentioned.

People did not discuss their troubles or problems when we were young, even to their closest friends. And they certainly never, ever discussed the weakness of family members. The only way I knew about Jane's parents is by what I could pick up from observation. I never once heard her say anything negative about them at all.

Still, I was aware that things were not right in her home, although I could not have expressed it; I just knew it.

Jane's mother was a very unhappy woman. You could see it in her face. She never smiled, that I can recall. Her lips seemed forever pinched in a thin line of disapproval, and there were deep frown lines between her eyes.

She was a fanatic about her house, always cleaning something. We could not touch a thing except in Jane's room. Once I picked up a magazine to look at the cover and I thought Jane was going to flip. She grabbed the thing from my hand and put it back on the table as if it were a piece of a prized puzzle, and had to fit just exactly so. "My mother doesn't want anything moved, not even a smidge!"

I laughed, halfway in embarrassment and halfway in disbelief, but the look of real fear on Jane's face shut me up immediately. She glanced furtively over her shoulder, as if to make sure her mother hadn't seen us, and shooed me quickly out of the room.

Her father was a handsome man, quite tall and slim, or so he seemed when I was young. He had a small moustache and thick curly black hair. The few times I saw him, he was quite charming to me, but he was gone all the time. I don't think I ever knew what he did.

Sometimes I wonder if Jane even knew. If so, she never told me. Then again, I don't think I was ever interested enough to ask.

My mum was poor, and we lived in a house that was always in need of repair, with faded, peeling paint and dingy wallpaper that had been there as long as I could remember, but she loved me and I knew it. And it was *our* house. Not just hers. Jane and I were welcome anywhere—my room, the living room, the dining room, the kitchen, even my mum's room when she was in it.

And I could touch anything I wanted. So could Jane.

I had no father, but I think I had a much happier childhood in spite of it. My mum smiled a lot, and giggled right along with us when we got silly.

We usually played at my house, but about every two weeks we'd have to go to Jane's for an afternoon. Her mother said it didn't look right to have her at my place all of the time. Now we don't have to worry about that anymore. Jane comes to my place always.

Jane's father disappeared right after she graduated from college, and her mother finally drank herself to death. Jane told me so, dry eyed, the day after she died. The papers called it heart failure. Jane sold the house, gave all the furniture to the Salvation Army, and never once looked back.

We're at the table, the first cup has been poured, and now I'll begin the ceremony of the gifts. I wish she wouldn't do this to me, this extravagance, this overwhelming-ness of giving. Even more, I wish I could enjoy it and not feel this whatever it is I feel. Unworthy perhaps, or perhaps it's because I can never repay. Never could, can't now, and never will be able to repay in kind.

Why do I still get fussed? It's way too late now. We've been doing this dance for ever so long and we're locked into the steps.

The gifts—a white silk blouse, a black cashmere sweater, an exquisite rich purple jewel-toned Hermes scarf—are the sort of things she always lavishes on me. But I am delighted as well as baffled by the huge box holding a dozen jars of Sicilian blood orange marmalade. That's a lifetime supply. Only Jane would do a thing like that.

Here's a list of the things you need for a proper tea:

1. Tea. Earl Grey is best. Never mind those namby-pamby flowery things. What you need is a stout, hearty tea with enough bones to pick you up and set you back on your feet, finish off your day with grace.
2. A small pitcher of milk. Not cream; cream is too heavy for tea.
3. A bowl of sugar cubes. Or, if you can afford it, Demerara sugar; those wonderful golden crystals are my favorite. They remind me of tropical island sands… not that I've ever really seen any.
4. Tongs for the sugar cubes and cloth napkins. Never, never, never use paper napkins.
5. A plate of cookies, homemade or the best store-bought you can afford. A few small sandwiches cut in strips or little triangles, no crusts. Mum used to butter both sides of the bread, then top the bottom piece with a thin slice of cucumber or little red-edged rounds of radishes. Lovely and crunchy.
6. Scones, hot from the oven. Slathered with orange marmalade. Oh heaven, if you can find the Sicilian blood orange marmalade. Never mind the cost; some things are above considering the cost. I've written down the

recipe for the scones. It's here somewhere where I've written down the rest of my recipes.

7. A freshly pressed tablecloth, pastels or white only. My favorite is the pale pink one that belonged to my Mum.
8. China teacups and your best teaspoons. No mugs. Mugs won't do for a proper tea. Tea is best shared with someone else. Someone you love is the first choice of course, but almost anyone can be pleasant company for half an hour or so. However, there are times when tea alone is exactly what you need. Then that makes:
9. Another person, except when you want to be alone.

Jane takes a long sip of her tea, sighs in contentment. She stretches her long legs out, like a sun-warmed cat, and wiggles her feet till her shoes fall off. She finally speaks.

"I've got something to tell you and I want you to behave yourself. No carrying on, do you understand? I'm the only one who is allowed to carry on. It's my job and I do it quite well if I do say so myself."

"You are not getting married again, are you? Tell me you're not going to do that stupid M word again, Jane. I couldn't stand it." She looks tired, I think. There's a darkness under her eyes that even her custom-blended make up can't hide.

"No, silly, I'm not going to get married. I'm going away. Actually I'm going into hiding and I'm not coming back out. I'm going away to die."

She holds up a perfectly manicured hand "Don't say anything. I've made up my mind, and there's nothing that will change it. I've been to the best oncologists around and they confirmed what I had already been told. Already knew, in my heart. I've got cancer in my lung. It started with breast cancer, but it's moved on now. It's a very aggressive type and the truth is I'm on my last lap."

I am stunned. My heart has stopped, as if I have been hit, hard, right in the middle of my chest. I try to speak, but there are no words, no breath to say them with.

"It's my own fault. I found a tiny lump in my breast well over a year ago, but decided it had to be just a small cyst, and chose to ignore it. I didn't have time in my life to be running to the doctor every time some little thing popped up."

"Jane! How could you? My God, Isn't there enough information about breast cancer? Every time you turn around there's an article, or an ad or *something* about it!" My breath has returned and with it, anger. How could she have done this?

"It's easy. You just refuse to acknowledge it. It doesn't exist, you see. I was too busy, too pressured, no time for medical problems. I wouldn't let myself think about it. I've had too many friends die of breast cancer, and I wasn't about to go through what they went through. Being chopped to pieces, pumped full of deadly poisons, losing all their hair, all of it. It's too painful, too horrible. And it scared me to death."

Her voice sounds strange, full of irony, "So that's exactly what happened. I was so afraid of the pain, and of maybe dying that I literally let myself be scared to death. You don't have to tell me how stupid I am. I've already told myself a million times."

"How do you know now?" Maybe she hasn't found out *everything*, maybe she just *thinks* she's dying. This whole conversation is unreal, crazy. If she pinched me right now, I wouldn't even feel it. "You've seen a doctor?"

"Dozens of 'em. I have been poked, prodded, peered at, and inspected from head to toe like a side of prime beef. I finally was forced to go because I had a nasty cough that was interfering with my acting. The director told me to go get it fixed because they were having to tape over and over. Right in the middle of scenes I'd start hacking away, and it was disrupting the filming. You can't do that for very long without somebody getting upset."

"What did they tell you?"

"Just what I'm telling you. The cancer has gone into my lung. I've already gone through one round of treatments, and it had no effect at all. It's growing really fast. I can choose to go through more treatments but the prognosis is the same, no matter what. It's over."

"It's over," echoes around the room and inside my head.

Jane is still talking, and I try to listen, try to understand her words,

"Dying is a messy business and I'm damned if I'm going to have a passel of people standing around weeping and wailing and watching me while I'm the one who's having to do the hard part. Perish the thought."

She laughs, but it's her stage laugh, I know it too well.

"I've taken a small cottage right smack beside my beloved ocean and hired a nurse companion to stay with me. No, I won't tell you where. It's all set. Written in stone, in a manner of speaking. Right down to the last act, and that one I'll play to an empty house, thank you very much."

Chapter Two

Jane taught me everything I ever knew about most of the fun stuff in life. She taught me how to flirt; how to laugh three different ways: the belly laugh, the girlish giggle, and the seductive laugh (she learned in her acting classes) and absolutely *everything* about sex.

God knows Mum never would have broached that taboo subject. I don't think I ever heard her even say the word *sex* in my whole life, much less have a discussion about it.

June 4, 1940

Dear Diary,

Jane spent the night last night and she told me some things I never heard before. About sex, and how people do it. I know she's not making it all up but I don't know how she finds all this weird stuff out. I know one thing for sure though, if that's what you have to do, I'm not going to do it. She says it's a lot of fun but she won't tell me if she has done it or not. It's disgusting.

About that time I discovered love. Or at least, what I thought was love, according to all the wonderful fairy stories I had read as a child.

My first, and as it turned out, my almost only love, Tom Tutweiler, was a classmate. He was quite good-looking, tall, and full of fun. He was always right in the middle of every bit of mischief the boys got into. He had curly blond hair that he was forever trying to plaster down, and beautiful blue eyes. He had the longest eyelashes I had ever seen on a boy. All the girls had major heart palpitations over him.

The fact that he was interested in me was the best part of the whole love thing. I was the envy of every girl in the school. My every waking moment was focused on him, and my fantasies at night were romantic dreams of passion turned loose. But no sex, of course.

November 12, 1940

Dear Diary,

Last night Tom Tutweiler and I necked for over an hour. He wanted me to do it but I told him I vowed to the Blessed Virgin Mary to go to my wedding a virgin and I certainly didn't intend to change my mind for him. I like necking all right but sometimes it leaves me feeling funny down there. Jane says it's how you feel when you are horny, but I don't want to do it with Tom, so how could I be horny? All I know is, I'm not going to do it with him, or anybody else for that matter. Unless maybe after I get married.

When I read that entry all these years later I have to smile. How naive I was, and how little I knew about human nature. Especially, how little I knew about my own body.

I had no idea how a look, a touch, could ignite a fire I never dreamed existed.

Foolish child, I never even noticed when all my innocence and high resolve flew right out the window of that car.

December 23, 1941

Dear Diary,

Rats. I did it. But never again. Tom and I parked

in his parent's garage last night because they were at some Christmas party they always go to. We had a couple of drinks of Scotch he snitched from his dad, then we necked for a while, which was fun but then he started messing around. I can't even bear to write where, and then he started doing it to me.

He said we were at war and who knows if we'd even live to get married and we had better do what we could while we had the chance. He was making so much noise I thought the whole neighborhood would hear us. It was a mess and I didn't think it was any fun at all but he said it was great. He got sort of mad at me because I didn't tell him when I was coming, but how the hell was I supposed to know? I never felt anything, anyway, that I know of.

At least it didn't take very long and if that's all there is to sex, you can count me out. I told Jane, and she says she is proud of me, now I am a woman. Really! Sometimes I can't belive what goes on in her mind!

Jane studies her teacup as though it's the most interesting thing in the room.

I am in shock, I think. Am I still breathing? This is preposterous, I think. She's putting on an act. No, it's not an act this time. I see the tears welling up in her eyes, spilling down her cheeks in streaks darkened with mascara.

"Oh, dammit, I was doing fine until now…." She carefully puts the cup down but I knock the table over reaching for her. I can hear everything. My heart and my beloved teapot are breaking.

We cry and she comforts me, patting me on the back, crooning softly, "It's all right, it's all right. Hush, baby, hush, hush."

God, this can't be happening. "Jane, I cannot believe this.

You have been my dearest friend for all my life. I cannot let you go away all alone. I can't bear the thought.

"Please, please, don't do this." I want to shake her, how could she have done such a thing? She's not stupid. Why did she let this happen?

She lifts her chin, setting her strong jaw in the stubborn, jutting manner I know so well, "It's done. And it's going to stay done. Please, if you love me as much as you say you do, then let me have my way. In the meantime…." she jumps up from the table.

"Good God, look at this mess, and oh crap, your teapot!"

Jane is as down to earth as anyone I have ever known but not given to vulgarity, and I begin to cry again. I stand there weeping like a ninny while she cleans up the wreckage.

"Listen, there's only a little time left in my life bank and I've already squandered all I intend to on sadness and anger. So tidy your face and let's go. You need a new tea set. We are going to have to find the most beautiful one that was ever made. And that, dear friend, will take some serious shopping. Blow your nose and get your coat."

She makes it clear that she is not going to talk about what's going on, about the illness, I mean. I cannot bear to say the word cancer. It's an ugly, hateful word, full of dread and doom and unspeakable pain.

As always, I do what she tells me. I wash my face, pat on fresh powder, and swipe at my eyes with the mascara brush. Jane is in the downstairs bath "refurbishing Broadway's very nearly most famous face," she always says.

"Don't you wish," my standard rebuttal.

Jane Potter Mayers Stoddard Smyth-Hinton Tetly (not the tea people, she is careful to point out) is not quite famous. But she is well known in the industry and is much in demand for important support parts. She is more than competent in her trade, known for

> *her subtle comedic skills. While she never appears to deliberately steal a scene, she has developed a certain presence that always manages to attract her share of attention. She is well-liked and respected by her peers.*

—(Copied from a review written in 1984 in the *New York Times*.)

Jane, oh Jane, how can I go on if you leave me? You are the light in my drab little corner, you are my candle in the darkness, my other self.

I am the self that would never dare, never dare to live beyond the safe, warm quiet of these few rooms, these few streets.

You are my escape, my magic ride to a world I can only know through you.

Please God, don't take her away. You don't need her, and I do. I pray. Please. Please. *Please.*

Chapter Three

Shopping with Jane is an experience. I always promise myself each time we go that this is the last time. I've been making that promise as long as I've known her and breaking it exactly as many times. It's difficult for me to imagine two women less alike in taste and style.

For myself, a nice navy blue whatever with a touch of white at the collar, or perhaps if it's a jacket and skirt, I'll add a pastel or dark paisley blouse.

For dress occasions I have a black silk crepe suit that I will never tire of. It's probably ten years old but it's perfectly good, a classic, and will never go out of style.

Jane, on the one hand, is convinced that if it glitters, it's great. She loves anything that twinkles or sparkles or glows in the dark. When we shop together she tries her best to "…liven you up, for God's sake, you look like a nun!"

I, on the *other* hand, am forever trying to convince her that it is not necessary to look like a neon beer sign to be well dressed.

Jane is looking for a teapot with rhinestones and I am looking for a teapot exactly like the one that's broken.

Right down to the stained spout and tiny hairline crack in the lid.

We wander aimlessly from store to store at the mall, never mentioning her illness or what is going to happen next. I feel as though I am in a trance, but wide awake. My mind whirls with questions, but the one I most want to ask, the only one that matters, I will not allow myself to fully form, even in my own mind.

We distract ourselves with banalities and little jokes about the tackiness of very nearly everything we see. As if everything was perfectly fine. How strange.

Finally, in the fine china department at Pendry's I see a lovely teapot. It's white, delicate, and sculpted to look like a small leafy cabbage. There's a sugar bowl and a cream pitcher, on their own oval tray, all done in the same cabbage pattern.

Jane sees it almost the same time I do.

"There it is, Ida Mae. It's perfect for you. There's your new teapot!" Can it be? Could we possibly be agreeing on the same thing? But I know in my heart she is choosing it for me because she will not be here to share it with me anyway.

And then the question gnaws its way into my mind, no longer willing to be buried, stuffed away in a dark corner where I can't see it,

"When? When are you going away?"

"Three weeks."

What? *Three weeks?* How can that be? How can a lifetime be over in three weeks? Jane grabs me by the arm. She is squeezing so hard it hurts.

"Hang on! Breathe! You look like you are about to faint. Don't you dare faint on me! I'll let you fall all over the floor and make a spectacle of yourself!"

February 17, 1942

Dear Diary,

I'm in love. We are in love. Tom is wonderful. He holds my hand when we are walking down the hall at school, and sometimes he kisses my fingertips. I could just melt. He tells me he's crazy about me a hundred times a day. Jane says it's not me he loves, it's all those fun body parts that I've got that he wants. I think she's jealous because I have Tom and she doesn't have anyone. The guys don't like her, Tom says, because she is too bossy and not sweet like me. I swear he'd do it ten times a day if I'd let him and we could find a place to hide.

Jane says I had better be very damn careful or I'll end up pregnant. God, I cannot let that happen. Mum would kill me, I'd have to leave school, and I'd be shamed forever. He got some of those rubber things from his older brother and he says it's okay, I can't get pregnant if he uses one.

February 28, 1942

Dear Diary

I'm so scared Tom will get drafted as soon as we get out of school, but he says we just have to live for today, and not worry. He says he's ready to go when they call him, but I think I'll die if he has to go away.

This war thing is so awful anyway. Brothers and sons and husbands and lovers and fathers all killing one another. It doesn't make any sense. If women ran the world, I'll bet there wouldn't be any war. I know I would never send anyone I loved off to be killed.

I don't know what's wrong with Mum. She cries at night when she thinks I can't hear her. I asked her if she was all right and she said yes, but sometimes she gets a little lonely. She loved my father she says. She wishes so hard that he had never gone on that business trip. Then he might not be dead today. But that was a long time ago, when I was a little baby, so I don't feel as sad about it as she does.

Still, sometimes I wish I had a father like everybody else. Except he might be like Jane's father, gone all the time, and I wouldn't be happy about that at all. Jane is going to be Juliet in the senior graduation play. She will be great; she looks like Juliet, and she is really good, even Tom has to admit it. I get to be in the crowd.

Walton Falls, the town I live in, is a *National Geographic* kind of place. Photographers come from all over the world to take pictures in the fall of the year. The rolling hills glow with rich reds and golds and brilliant yellows. My street is especially beautiful then, when the trees make a tunnel of sunlight filtered through the dusty turning leaves.

The white, mostly Victorian houses, so grand once upon a time, are a little seedy now, but still beautiful, with wide, welcoming porches and open doors that to this day are rarely locked. The town is small, smaller now than in the 1800s, when it was a thriving mill town.

But that was a long time ago, and now it's just another sleepy little farm village outside Cincinnati. Close enough for those few determined souls who are willing to make the long drive to work and still too far for all the bad influences that big city living bring. The high school usually graduates between forty and fifty children, just as it did when we went there.

And like most small towns, football is always a big deal. Friday night games are a major social event. Even though the school hasn't won much in years. We still troop down to the old field that they have been playing on since the game first came to town. This year they just might win. Or maybe next year or the next. The hope never dies. One day we will win. I hope I'm here to see it.

March 23, 1942

Dear Diary,

Three more months till graduation. I can't wait!!!!!!! Mum and I have talked it over and there's no way she can afford to send me to college.

I'm going to have to get a job and maybe I can save enough to go to secretarial school in a year or so. That's fine with me because I don't want to be away from Tom anyway. I love him and we are going to get married in two years, war or no war (that's Tom's and my secret; I have not told Mum yet).

Jane is going to New York to study drama. She is determined to be an actress; she wants it more than anything. She says she will never get married because it would interfere too much with her acting career and her career is her life. Her parents think that she is going to study to be a drama teacher. They would die if they knew the truth. She says even if they find out, once she is famous they'll get over it, and then they'll be proud of her.

I really admire her: I could never do the things she does, like going so far away all alone and being around people she doesn't know, but she says she can't wait. Oh well, that's the difference between us.

March 30, 1942

Dear Diary,

Aunt Germaine is making Bernadette go to Radcliffe. They came to tea yesterday. Aunt G. was so snotty about me not being able to go away to school, it made me mad. She was trying to make Mum feel bad, I know.

Mum starts to fidget and fiddle with her hair when Aunt Germaine starts with her ever-so-subtle criticism. She makes the meanest things sound so mild until you think about it. She told Mum it was a shame she was not in a position to take care of me too, since Mum had so little to manage on. But then, she said, I suppose that Ida Mae will be perfectly happy with a nice simple job, anyway. Mum jumped up from the table and stormed into the kitchen without a word, but we could see that she was really mad. Her face was as red as a beet.

Bernadette and I looked at each other and decided it was a good time to go for a walk. When we left, Mum was standing at the back door with her arms crossed, staring out at the garden. I think it's the first time Bern and I ever talked honestly to each other. I feel sorry for her. She told me she would run away if she could. She does not want to go away to that stupid school; she says she is in love with Billy Taylor, but her mother won't even let her say his name in their house because he is just a mechanic, and besides he has a little bit of a club foot, so he walks funny and Aunt G thinks he is terrible.

Poor Bern. Funny, I never used to like her, but now I feel sorry for her.

April 2, 1942

Dear Diary,

Aunt Germaine and Bern came to dinner today, after they went to church. They go to the richest church in town, of course, and we go just down the street. After dinner Bern and I sat on the front steps and she told me a secret that I can't tell anybody in the whole wide world, ever. She says that her mother cheats for all those prizes she wins at the state fair for her ever-so-great orange marmalade!!!! Can you believe it? Bern says she orders the marmalade from a store in New York City, they send it to her, and then she puts it in her own jars!!!!!! Ha, Ha, Ha!!! The old cheat!

If it's difficult to imagine two women as unlike one another as Jane and I are, it's even more difficult to imagine my mother and Aunt Germaine as sisters.

Mum, rather short, with dark brown curly hair and a beautiful smile, was reserved in both her demeanor and dress. Not shy, really, just not effusive. I suppose I am like her in many ways. Mum's idea of makeup was a light pink lipstick, and the barest dusting of face powder. That's good enough for me, too. I am told I look very much like her, and sometimes, when I look in the mirror just so, I almost think I can see her.

Aunt Germaine was the exact opposite. She was tall, and had long blond (straight from a bottle) hair that she wore swooped up on top of her head like a crown. She wore every kind of face paint on the market. She dressed most elegantly, always in very expensive outfits. She somehow managed to make sure we knew how much they cost, so we could appreciate how well off she was. She had to be the center of attention, and was on every board and club in town.

It's hard to believe that the two women came from the same set of parents. Mum was younger by three years. I never heard them have a real argument, but every once in a while you could feel the chill in the room. They would speak to one another, stiff and formal, like strangers at a social gathering. And then sometimes they would laugh for hours over nothing.

Germaine married when she was twenty-seven, very late by the standards of the day, and the man she married was considerably older than she was. But he had tons of money, that was very carefully and clearly implied, and when he died he left her quite well off. It did not bring her happiness. As far as I can tell, nothing did.

Mum married for love. At least that's what she always told me. My father was a photographer. He went around from town to town taking pictures of families and weddings and businessmen.

He was killed tragically in a freak car accident two months after I was born. Mum had only one picture of him, and several times as a child I caught her holding that fading photo and crying.

I often wondered what he would have been like to me if he had lived. Mum says he would have loved me dearly, and the happiest day of his life was the day I was born. But, I'll never really know.

June 11, 1942

Dear Diary,

That's it! School is over forever! I am so glad! Tom and I could not go to the dance because he didn't have any money, and neither did I, so we went out to River Park to have our own little private party.

Tom said we can have just as much fun by ourselves as we can cramming into that hot gym, stuffed into clothes we don't like anyway. He didn't want to wear a tux from the beginning, but I felt really sad about missing the dance, and not having a beautiful formal like all the other girls. Even Jane had a date, and she begged me to go double with her but I couldn't do that to Tom.

I could tell he'd been drinking the minute he picked me up, and once we got to the park he got really smashed. He wanted to do it but he couldn't make that damn thing stay hard and then he fell asleep on top of me. I thought I'd be smushed before I pushed him off onto the floor of the car. I didn't care if he broke his neck! After he woke up (finally) we had a big fight, and he threw up twice, so it was not a very fun graduation.

June 15, 1942

Dear Diary,

We made up today. These last few days have been horrible. I have been so sad, and lonely. Tom was really sorry and he's being a darling again. When he looks at me with those big blue eyes, and begs me not to be mad at him, I just can't resist. He runs around me like a silly puppy and pulls at my dress and acts goofy till I have to laugh. At least school is over and now I can start looking for a job.

The good news is, Tom is not going to be drafted after all. He had rheumatic fever when he was six and got a heart murmur from it. The doctor says it's nothing to worry about, but he can't go into the service. Tom says he wanted to do his part for the war effort, but I don't care, I am so happy I could flip! He is going to trade school to learn to be a pressman, and stay right here with me. I bet he'll be great at it, too.

Jane has always had absolute power over me. If she says such and such makes her feel sad, I immediately feel sad. If she is bubbling with happiness, I am happy too. Have I any emotions that are mine alone? I wonder.

After we were a little older I began to share even the most intimate moments of my life with her and take hints about my feelings from her reactions.

Years later, only after she became indignant about Tom's drinking, did I begin to recognize the anger I had stuffed away into the deepest parts of my mind. That anger, and her never ending support, gave me the courage to re-claim my life.

Now we stand together in the fine china department and I am lost. I am lost. Our lives are so deeply interwoven, to remove one of us from the tapestry we have spent a lifetime creating tears at the very core of us both.

We buy the teapot. Jane pays for it while I trail along behind her obediently. I will not faint. I will not make a spectacle of myself because it would embarrass her. Would it embarrass me? I doubt it. If it would remove me from the face of the earth I might even welcome it.

"Come on." She pulls me after her. "You'll be fine. You are a strong woman, after all. Look, let's face it, there's nothing new or unusual about what's happening to me. Everybody gets their turn sooner or later. Mine is just sooner than yours." She giggles, and her nose crinkles in that funny way she has had ever since we were little girls, "I always was a step ahead of you. Why should it be any different now?"

That's true. Jane was the leader and I was her willing follower from the first day we met. Why should it be different now?

We leave the store and return to the darkening house.

I turn on lights, unwrap my new teapot, and place it in the center of the dining room table, and beside it the charming little sugar bowl and creamer on the cabbage leaf tray. It is lovely. So white and perfect on the gleaming mahogany wood. It's thinner walled than my mum's teapot, and I find myself wondering if it will keep the tea hot enough.

"My plans are to return to New York for a few days, finish getting my affairs in order, that sort of thing, then I'll be back. I won't stay here. You know how I am about my privacy. I'll stay at the hotel and we'll spend all our days together. It'll be fun. You get your thinking cap on, plan some pleasant things to do. Not too strenuous though. I do tend to tire a little easier than I used to.

"And I don't want to tell Kate and Jenny, or even Bern. I want to take the memory of our happy times with me on my trip."

"Jane! You'll break their hearts! Kate would be

devastated, and you know it. You've got to tell them sometime, even if it's only a day or two before you leave."

She sighs, and nods. Her face is a mask; she is ever the actress, in full control of her emotions. "I know you're right. I don't want to, but I'm sure Kate would never forgive me if I went off without saying goodbye. It's going to be so hard. I absolutely dread it, but I'll do it anyway. But we'll wait till just before I leave, okay?"

What can I do? I nod agreement. My eyes are burning too, with tears that I dare not spill. If I start to cry now, I'll never stop again.

Jane is watching me, her head tilted to one side, from the dining room doorway, and I'm not about to let my weak nature betray me. If she wants me to be strong, I'll be the strongest woman in the Western hemisphere, by God!

"I'll call my social secretary first thing in the morning, and we'll plan the itinerary, madam."

Then, the grand exit. More whirling and kisses, a gust of cold air, and Jane is gone.

I am alone in my house.

Chapter Four

After Jane leaves my days seem to pass as if I am underwater. I cry. I cry until I wonder where one more tear can come from. And there are flashes of anger, no, rage, at what is happening. How could she have done this to herself? To me? It isn't fair!

Jane is beautiful and talented, no question. And she is proud of her looks and skills. I would be too, in her shoes. I've always known she was a bit vain, but this goes way beyond vanity. To refuse to take care her life because of her looks is impossible for me to understand. I'll not even try. My heart is broken, and there's nothing I can do about it.

But my daily work gets done somehow, and my life, to a visitor from Mars, would appear to be going on quite normally. I move through the rooms of my house, making the bed, washing, drying, and putting up the dishes, dusting where I can see it needs it, all the chores that one does over and over and over until they are such a deeply ingrained habit that by the end of the day I don't even remember what I've done.

My house was built in 1860. I've lived in it all my life, except for that dreadful time in the cold-water flat.

After Mum died I inherited it, lock, stock, and barrel.

She had very little money left, poor thing, and I think that's why she was reluctant to see a doctor. The house is old and cold and drafty as a chicken coop. But it's mine, and the main reason I've been able to survive is because, drafty or not, it's paid for.

I love this place, chilly corners and all. The rooms are huge, and the ten-foot ceilings make them seem even bigger.

Every room has an elegant fireplace, with a beautifully

carved wood mantel. Except for the gas grate in the living room fireplace, not one of them is usable, but they look great. The mirrors over them are darkened and cracked. Sometimes I wonder what scenes live on in those ancient reflections.

Of all the rooms, I enjoy my bedroom—which used to be my mother's—and my kitchen. The bedroom is a long room, almost the length of two, with plenty of space near the floor-to-ceiling windows for an only slightly shabby fainting couch, covered in pale cream damask, like a fine lady who has seen better times, and a small table and lamp. In the spring I see the trees budding out before almost anyone except the birds.

The kitchen has seen who knows how many women preparing a million meals and more for their families and friends and relatives. What stories must live among the dishes in the tall old white cabinets, and around the heavy oak table that has stood in the center of the room forever.

That table must have been built right in the room, because it's much too big to fit through any of the doors.

But of course, of all the rooms, the sunroom, with windows all around and green things growing inside and out, is my most favorite place of all. Except in the heart of winter, then it's entirely too damp and cold, even on sunny days.

Over the years I've spent some money on the house, mostly for necessary repairs. All my plans for remodeling, re-doing, and exotic restorations remain to this day tucked neatly away in the desk drawer. I haven't looked at them in years. Now the burden and/or the pleasure will fall on my daughter, Kate, if she decides she wants to keep this old mausoleum after I die.

So many memories of Kate dwell here. Her childish laughter, and squeals of delight still echo throughout the rooms. She loved playing hide-and-seek with Jane, running from room to room in a frenzy of excitement. Her dark hair tumbling into gleeful eyes, her little bare feet slapping on the wooden floors. She couldn't bear to stay hidden for more than a minute or two, and even with her baby hands pressed tightly over her mouth, you could hear her half a house away.

Jane used every bit of her acting repertoire to become a dragon, a winged fairy, a hunched-over troll, or a wonderful magical princess, changing roles before our amazed eyes. Kate was, and still is, crazy about her. There is nobody quite like her Aunt Jane.

The best part of living in such an old house is the history, the known and the unknown. The breath, the tears, and the laughter of a hundred others share this place with me. Now I'm adding to the tears.

I'm sure I've worked harder than I ever have in my life, but as long as I keep moving, I can keep on living. Or so it seems to me.

Maybe I learned that from Mum and Aunt Germaine. When they stopped, they died.

September 6, 1942

Dear Diary,

Well, Aunt Germaine won first place at the fair again for her stupid orange marmalade. She waves that piss-ant little blue ribbon around like she's won the biggest prize in the world. I just wonder what she'd do if I told the truth about what she does.

Boy! That would sure fix Mrs.-I'm-Better-Than-Everybody, wouldn't it! I won't though, only because it would embarrass my darling Mum and I'd rather have my fingernails pulled out than do that. I wish I could figure out some way to hint to Aunt G., kind of leave her wondering whether I know or not, and if I do will I tell. Now that would be great revenge!

I had a bad time this past week, I was late with my period, about ten days, and it scared me something fierce! I told Tom but he said there was no way; he always uses one of those rubber things. He acted as if it was all my fault somehow. Anyway, it finally got here. I had terrible cramps and it was a really heavy one but who cares, I had one, and that's what counts.

September 21, 1942

Dear Diary,

Yippee! I have a new job at the print shop. I am so excited. I hope Tom will come to work here too, when he gets through trade school. The war effort needs someone here at home to do the printing, so I told Tom he's doing his part after all. I'm learning how to do pasteup and stuff like that. It's what you do to get typesetting ready for the printer, then he makes a negative and burns a plate from that. Do I sound like I know what I'm doing or what? It's lots of fun, and Mr Berry, my boss, says I'm very good at it. I am so happy.

The ritual of my afternoon tea, the preparation and the warm comfort of the first sip keep me anchored in the present. The past is only a dreamy memory, and the future bodes no good. The present moment, right now, is all I can handle.

When I was young, tea time was my favorite time of the day, even though occasionally I would grumble when Mum called me in from a particularly interesting bit of play with my friends.

Still, I loved it. Mum allowed me to pick from her collection of handpainted china cups, a different one each day, and the time spent with her in such a loving and cozy atmosphere was better than anything I could concoct with my playmates. It was our own private ritual.

Then, over the years the ritual changed. It became a habit. Habits can be beneficial or not, but either way they are automatic. Habits do not require that one be aware. One derives no pleasure (or pain) from a habit because there is no one there to notice.

And so it was with my tea time in those difficult days. I still had tea each day, more or less at four in the afternoon, but in truth I could not tell you five minutes after I finished what I had or how it tasted. I felt no comfort, no sense of pleasure from what had once been the best part of the day for me.

After I grew older, for reasons I cannot explain, gradually tea time began again to become an important part of my day. Once again I began to pay attention and once again I began to feel the comfort, the satisfaction, that I had learned to enjoy many years before.

I suppose it's because, as one grows older, one has to deal with pain that cannot be ignored. Sometimes it seems that life is mostly pain with very little pleasure to be found anywhere.

It's then that comforting little rituals become one's saving grace in otherwise bleak times. If nothing else, there's always those few quiet minutes when all we have to do is enjoy the taste of the steaming tea, the sweetness of a good orange marmalade or tart raspberry jam on a warm scone.

For a few peaceful moments time stops and one finds enough courage to finish the day.

I must come to grips with what is happening to Jane. I have no idea how. I simply cannot fathom life without her in it. Now she tells me I must. God knows I've dealt with death before. I was an infant when my father died. I cannot feel much grief about that, but losing my mother was a dreadful experience.

Even to this day, sometimes I miss my mum. And losing Tom, even though he's not dead, was so painful. And of course, Robert broke my heart in a thousand pieces. I don't think it ever really completely mended after him. Perhaps that's why there's never been another man in my life. Once burned, twice shy, I suppose.

Still, somehow that all seemed to be in the normal course of a life. Parents die, husbands and wives and even the most ardent of lovers part, through death or other natural causes, and the survivor suffers for a while, then picks up the pieces and gets on with it.

But Jane is different. Jane is my connection. Through her I experience a world in which I would never have had the courage to live single-handedly. She brings excitement and glamour and drama to me, presenting them in many-colored pictures painted with a thousand words.

Jane. I think if she dies half of me dies too. And yet, I'm not ready to die. I want to be with my precious daughter and my beloved granddaughter at least a little while longer.

I haven't seen my last spring, nor have I shared my last cup of tea on a rainy afternoon.

Even if half of me is gone there's another half still left, and Jane would be furious with me if I were to give up my joy in life simply because she isn't here to prompt me.

I must find a way to get through this. I must get over the anger. It's too late for anger, now.

Even more, I must find a way somehow, to learn to live on without my best friend. She expects no less, and I will not disappoint her.

Chapter Five

Life goes on. That's my new mantra. Will it work? I have no way of knowing. I just keep on rolling it over and over in my mind like a stone, hoping that it will take on some reality for me eventually.

Life does indeed go on, and I am preparing tea for Kate and Jenny this afternoon as I have hundreds of afternoons before.

Jenny has always loved the pecan lacy cookies I make, so of course I prepare a huge batch. Some to crunch on at tea and extra for her to take home. You never know when you are going to need a cookie or two. It's always best to have a few on hand.

They arrive late, as usual, scattering little piles of snow and puddles of water on my freshly polished hall floor.

Kate has never been able to understand the concept of the front hall rug. She drips all over the floor, then puts one foot on the rug, using it to mop up what she could have just as easily left on it to begin with. Jenny knows what I am thinking. She looks at me and winks. *That's my mom*, her wink says, *but we love her, don't we?*

My Kate. My beloved daughter. I see so much of me in her, her dark hair and ready smile, and that charming (at least to me) little sideways look she has. And yet, so much of her is totally unique that I wonder where this marvelous stranger came from.

March 18, 1943

Dear Diary,

I'm in terrible trouble. I'm pregnant. No doubt about it. I've missed two periods, my breasts are so sore I can hardly touch them, and Jane says that is as good a sign as any. It must have happened New Year's Eve. We both had way too much to drink and Tom refused to use a rubber. He says it's not the same with one on and he talked me into it. I have to admit it didn't take a lot of talking.

Now here I am. I can't tell Mum. She is sick. She is tired all the time, and lays on the couch curled up under a raggedy old quilt. I have begged her to go to the doctor but she says it's not anything to worry about, she'll be fine when the weather gets warmer. I do worry about her though, she looks like she is getting thinner by the day and I am scared to death. Now on top of all this, here I am. Tom knows. He says he doesn't care, but he acts like he is angry. When I ask him if he is mad, he snaps at me not to pester him.

We will just have to go ahead and get married earlier than we planned. I wanted to wait till I was twenty, but I guess eighteen will have to do. With him in school we'll have to live on my salary and I don't know how we will manage but Tom says we can do it.

I guess we'll get married in May and I'm going to have to not look pregnant till after the wedding. I wish I felt happier about all this but I don't. And I don't even feel like trying.

I remember, in a muffled sort of way, how stricken I was when I finally had to face the fact that I was pregnant. I was so very young, and felt absolutely alone. I had no one to confide in. Certainly not my mother. I was dead certain she would not stop loving me but I had judged myself, and was too ashamed to tell her. Jane knew, but even with her, I could not bring myself to talk about it. And yet, in spite of the fear and sadness, I wanted that baby. Perhaps somehow, I already knew what the future held.

May 17, 1943

Dear Diary,

Well here I am. A married woman. We got married on my birthday, two days ago, which I thought would be fun but it was a disaster instead. Aunt Germaine could not get over how much weight I've gained and she harped on it all day. I think she has guessed. I really don't care, but she sure wore it out.

Mum is not any better, in fact, I think she's worse. Sometimes when I talk to her I can tell she is not hearing a word I say. I tried to talk to Aunt Germaine and she ignored me too. Nobody will listen to me. Mum did look very pretty at the wedding in her new pink dress, everybody said so.

I wore a white lace suit that I got on sale at Benninton's. I must admit I felt a pang of guilt about that. I most certainly wasn't qualified for white. It was a pretty outfit, but the skirt was so tight by the end of the wedding I thought I was going to strangle. I bought it only three weeks before especially so it would still fit. Oh well, missed on that one.

It was a small wedding. Bernadette (ugh) was my bridesmaid because Jane could not afford to come all the way from New York. (I was awfully disappointed about that, too.) She wore a pale green dress and I guess she looked okay. Billy sure seemed to think so; he stared at her like a tomcat stalking a mouse during the whole ceremony.

We had only family. Tom has a big family; four brothers, two sisters, their spouses, his mother and father, and about six hundred relatives. At least it seemed that way.

The worst thing about the whole wedding was that Tom and Billy got into a fist-fight right there in the church parlor. It was horrible. Billy started it because he thought Tom was making fun of him because he's 4F on account of his foot (why, I don't know, since Tom's 4F, too), and Tom hit him back. Punched him smack in the nose. Then the little creep stood there right over the punch bowl dripping blood into the Summer Wedding Punch. It was hard enough getting extra sugar ration stamps for the cake and punch, then they had to go and spoil it. I was so mad I could hardly stand it.

They had both been out in back drinking and I know they were at least a little drunk, I don't care what Tom says. Anyway, Bern took Billy outside to clean him up and by then everyone was in a big hurry to leave. Naturally, Aunt Germaine was in a real snit. I did not speak to Tom until this morning. We are off to a great start.

Then I had tell my mother that I was pregnant. I still think it was the hardest thing I ever had to do in my life. I knew she would not be mean to me about it, but I also knew it would disappoint her deeply.

I waited until about a week after the wedding. Late one afternoon I knew I could not put it off another minute.

Mum was resting on the couch—she looked so little under that faded old quilt—I sat down on the floor beside her, and laid my head on the soft mound of her body.

"Mum, I have to tell you..." And then the tears started.

"Ida Mae, what on earth...?" Her hand smoothed my hair, but I could feel the tremor in it. "What is it, child?"

"Mum, I'm... I'm pregnant!" I wailed.

For the tiniest moment she looked angry. She had a way of frowning, eyes narrowing, that I had known since childhood. My heart stopped for a beat, then she reached for me, and took me in her arms. Holding me so tightly I could hardly breathe.

We cried together.

All the fear and hurt and sorrow poured out of me in great racking sobs. My mum held me like she had when I was a little girl and had fallen off my bike, rocking me and saying over and over, "It's all right, my precious, it's all right, it's all right". I knew it wasn't, and our lives never would be the same again, but her words comforted me and finally we both dried our tears.

Then, of course, as women have always done after such an emotional experience, we got the giggles. I told her about how tight my wedding dress had been and how miserable I was the whole time, and that the waist button had popped off halfway through the very brief service, and we giggled about that.

We very nearly fell off the sofa laughing about the way Aunt Germaine looked when the fight started.

It was all right after all. Different, but still all right.

We agreed that Mum would tell Aunt Germaine. What a relief that was! I most ardently did not want to face her with this kind of news. Mum never told me what she said, but she must have made it clear to her sister in no uncertain terms to be nice to me, because Aunt G. simply said she was not surprised, and that she hoped I'd have a healthy baby. What a huge relief to have that over with.

July 24, 1943

Dear Diary,

I am so miserable. This is the worst mistake I have ever made in my life. We have no money, I am tired all the time, and all we can afford is this awful cold-water flat to live in. It's dark and dirty and I'm too tired to do anything about fixing it up.

Tom doesn't care. He never gets home till around eight o'clock. He has to stop and have a few beers after school. He says it's because they study, but what can you study in a bar about running a press I'd like to know. He tries to start that silly game of pulling at my dress and begging me not to be mad at him, but it's not so funny anymore.

And I don't have the proper stuff to make my tea. I have to use tea bags and a nasty old mug with a chip on the edge and I don't even have a teapot. Just a dented screechy kettle that I have to heat the water in over an electric hot plate. Jane is too far away, we can never talk anymore. I miss her ever so much.

I hate it and I hate Tom and I wish I was dead sometimes. Except when the baby moves, then I don't want to be dead because I love my baby already, and I can't wait to hold it in my arms.

July 27, 1943

Dear Diary,

Mum is really sick. Aunt Germaine took her to the doctor yesterday and he put her in the hospital the minute he saw her. I am praying my heart out every minute for her to get well. I don't know how to take care of a baby and I need her. I can't get anyone to tell me what's wrong with her. They tell me not to worry, it's not good for the baby.

I pretended to be convinced that she would get well. I sat with her every day, in her darkened room. She said the brightness hurt her eyes, so we kept the curtains pulled, with only one dim lamp over in the corner for me to see by. She was too sick to talk much, but after she got her pain shots she felt a little better for a short time, and then we'd talk about the baby and all the fun we'd have after it was born.

Mum held my hand a lot, and she never once let on, but we knew. The truth hung between us like a wall we didn't know how to get over. I sat by her bed in a straight-back chair till my back hurt so badly I couldn't sit there another second. There was a small couch in the room, and I would move over there till my back eased a bit, then I'd go back to the bedside.

We were there for a week. I was sitting on the couch when she died.

August 10, 1943

Dear Diary,

My mother died of cancer on August 2, 1943, at two in the afternoon. I was with her. One minute she was alive, my mum, and the next minute she was gone forever. She was buried in the pink dress she wore to my wedding, at Calvary Cemetery on August 4, 1943, at eleven in the morning.

Goodbye, my darling mother.

Your loving daughter,

Ida Mae.

For a long time I could not think about it. I moved through the days like a puppet.

Tom was worse than useless. I needed him to hold me, but he backed off every time I tried. He left me night after night after night, sitting alone, staring into space. Wishing myself dead.

Finally, the first awful weeks passed and I began to come around. The baby flipped and flopped and bubbled around in my belly. A baby who would soon be needing me. It was my turn to be the mother. I had a wonderful reason to go on in spite of my loss.

We moved back into the house and I painted and prettied up my old room for the baby's nursery.

I had no way of knowing, until my daughter had her child, what I had missed. How could I? You cannot miss what you never had to begin with.

It was so grand to be there for Kate, even if only to listen to her gripe about how tired she was, and how the baby kept her up all night. I am everlastingly grateful that I can share my daughter's life as an adult. It's one of the best parts of being a mother.

Growing older turns out, much to my surprise, to have all sorts of advantages I could not see when I was Kate's age. It's really quite nice. Most of the time.

September 27, 1943

Dear Diary,

My beautiful, precious baby girl was born on September 10, 1943 at two in the afternoon. Isn't that wonderful? She is perfect. I have named her Kate Ellen after Mum. No time to write more, I am very busy with her.

Learning to be a mother seemed to come naturally, although there were certain technical details, like how to fold a diaper so it would fit that miniscule bottom, and how to hold her safely for her first tub bath, secrets of the trade that I had to rely on Aunt Germaine for. The loving part came with the baby. I lost my heart the minute I laid eyes on her.

November 6, 1943

Dear Diary,

I keep trying to take the time to catch up in here but it never seems to happen. My baby is such a joy, I haven't got the words to describe her. I adore her. I don't think I could have ever imagined such a perfect little body, and her wiggle-all-over smiles.

She is a very happy baby, thank God, because I have no clue about how to take care of her. Aunt Germaine comes over about once a week and she really tries to help but she is terribly bossy and I have a hard time trying to be as grateful as I know I should be. Tom thinks Kate is cute but doesn't really have that much to do with her. He won't hold her, he says he's scared he'll drop her. How silly! If I insist, and put her in his arms he sits like a carved statue, not moving a muscle, not even his mouth, till he whispers to take her, take her, please!

I am sure he'll get over it when she is older, but it makes me sad. I want him to love her as much as I do.

December 1, 1943

Dear Diary,

Jane calls me every few weeks. Good thing, too, I know she can't afford it, but she is my only best friend and I need her more than ever. She is the one person in the world I can talk to. I miss my Mum. Sometimes I miss her so much I hurt all over. I cry every time I think of her and I think of her every day. God, I wish she was here to see my baby. She would be so proud.

I feel like throwing a great big temper tantrum and screaming and crying. I want my mum! I want my mum! But there's nobody I can turn to. Except my dear Jane and she's not here. Still, I know she cares, and she'll get here as soon as she can.

Kate and Jenny stay until almost six. You would think that after spending most of every day planning, preparing, and serving tea to half a hundred women and squealy little girls the last thing in the world they would want to do is sit down with an old lady and have more tea. But we get together for our lifelong ritual at least once a week.

What a joy they are, these two young women, my daughter and her daughter. Kate grows more lovely every year. Her dark hair has a few strands of gray now, which she refuses to dye. She has always looked way younger than her age, and now it's really starting to pay off.

Jenny is even prettier than her mother was at that age, if such a thing is possible. She has gone blond, (shades of her great-aunt Germaine!) and is the most self-possessed young woman I have ever had the good fortune to know. I don't believe in reincarnation, but still, I swear she has been here before. She is exceptionally wise for her age.

Even so, I have a hard time remembering she is an adult now. I have a great deal of respect and deep love for her, but inside there's a bit of longing for the little girl who was always so happy to see me she would run and fling her arms around my legs with all her tiny energy. I'd have to struggle for balance.

Einstein was right about time being relative. The good times fly by in a blur. The bad times seem to drag, one dreadful second after the other, in terrible slow motion

Jenny grew up in a blur of good times. All arms and legs and mischievous grins. Birthday cakes and bikes, heaps of books and a room full of giggling girls spin past my eyes in a kaleidoscope of memories.

I suppose that's why I still always make extra cookies for her to take home. She may be grown up to everyone else, but to me, the child still lives. She manages the tearoom, charms all the customers, and generally is a delight to be around. Kate and I are truly in awe of her.

After they leave I sit in the warm glow of lamplight and love, and weep slow, happy tears. Life has been hard, it's true.

But oh, look what I've got.

Chapter Six

Jane is the vital force in our long friendship. I have never been able to figure out why she stayed close to me when her own life was such wonderful high drama. No matter how busy or exciting her life is, no matter where she is in the world, we talk every few weeks. Her phone bills must be horrendous. She won't let me call.

"You've got better things to do with your money. Put it away for our baby girl, I'll make the calls," she tells me every time I mention it.

Several times a year she comes to visit, slashing through town like a comet, trailing stars and small planets in her wake.

July 6, 1945

Dear Diary,

Jane is in the USO! She is traveling all over Europe entertaining the troops at American bases and having a fabulous time. She is meeting some famous stars who come overseas to do shows with her unit, and she loves every minute of it. I'd be scared to death. When she becomes rich and famous too, "our Kate" (that's what she calls her) will have the best of everything. I hope so, because we are still struggling along on not near enough. If it wasn't for being in this house I don't know what we'd do.

Tom is having a very difficult time of it. He hates his job, and it's the third one he's had this year. He just can't seem to find one he likes and I am afraid he's drinking way too much for his own good. I think maybe he feels bad because he didn't get into the service. If I dare to say anything about it to him he gets very angry. I know he's having a difficult time, still it seems to me that all that drinking isn't helping any.

I'm trying very hard to love him and be an understanding wife, but to tell the truth sometimes I wish he had been drafted, then I wouldn't be in all this mess.

That summer was one of the worst on record. The humidity and the temperature were often the same, both very high, and Kate was covered with an awful heat rash.

Even as uncomfortable as she must have been she was in love with the world. She laughed at everything, kept me going, and truly was the only thing that made my life worthwhile.

September 15, 1945

Dear Diary,

Aunt Germaine has been found out!!! I feel ever so sorry for her. She has been embarrassed utterly. Last Tuesday the mailman delivered a large package to her while she was standing out in front of her house talking to Mrs Miller, Mrs Herkimer, and several other ladies who had been at some kind of a church meeting there and were getting ready to leave.

Well, the package had been damaged in the mail, I guess, and right before all those women, big jars of marmalade spilled out and smashed all over the sidewalk. I'm sure she wanted to die on the spot but the truth was all over the ground in a big gooey mess for God and all the world to see! Then as if that wasn't enough to bring down poor old Germaine, two days later we found out that Bernadette has left school to elope with Billy the unacceptable mechanic.

It's funny, I thought I would get a big kick out of Aunt G's cheating at marmalading being revealed and Bern defying her mother's stuffiness but I find that all I feel is very sorry for the old woman. She never meant any harm, she just wanted to be the best at something but never knew how. Poor thing.

November 11, 1945

Dear Diary,

Jane's tour with the USO is finished and she says she is worn to a nub. She will be home in a few days to rest and lick her wounds, then she is thinking of going back to London to see what's left of theater there. I hope she changes her mind. I don't want her to be that far away ever again. I just thank God that nightmare war is over. And even if I do get upset with Tom, I am grateful that he didn't have a part in all that ugliness.

December 12, 1945

Dear Diary,

I just found out poor Bern is living in a rundown trailer house on the edge of town with Billy and working as a waitress at the Bon-Ton Eatery and Aunt Germaine has gone into hiding. She doesn't even go the grocery store anymore. She has her stuff delivered.

I go to visit her once in a while and she seems to enjoy seeing the baby. Of course, who wouldn't. She is perfectly adorable. Even Tom gets a kick out of her. When he's sober. He likes to cuddle her on his lap and sing to her, he swears she understands every word.

The sad part is, he's not there most nights, till too late to see her at all. I don't know what to do about his drinking. He promises and promises but the longest he has gone is a few days. I know he's under a lot of stress and I try not to fuss, still, it's very hard to live with.

May 15, 1946

Dear Diary,

I finally made it to twenty-one! Now I am officially grown-up. It's funny, I feel as though I've been a grown-up for a hundred years, with a baby, this house, and my job. Jane is the smart one. She is having a grand time in Europe, traveling all over.

She sends me the most beautiful postcards I have ever seen and she writes wonderful long letters telling me all about her experiences. She sent me a photo of her standing smack in the middle of some very important bridge in London, arms flung wide, laughing into the camera, as if to say, "Here's my bridge!" I love reading her letters; it's like getting my own private adventure novel in installments. I miss her ever so much but I'm happy for her too.

She misses "our Kate" and asks about her in every letter. She says she has bought her some fabulous toys and dresses which she will send for Christmas. I guess that means she will not be here. I haven't asked because I don't want to know, not yet. That way I can keep hope alive a little longer. I really need her. I have no one to talk to and I'm so lonely.

Jane did not come home that year. I spent much of my time at the library, volunteering to read Christmas stories to the children, always with Kate tucked up on my lap. The new year was no better than the year before. I worked. Mrs Cox, who had lived next door forever, was the world's best baby sitter. Kate was perfectly happy to go to her house.

Good thing too, because one of us had to keep a steady job. Tom complained constantly. He didn't like his boss, he didn't like his work, the people he worked with were all out to give him a hard time. He was fired once, and laid off twice during the year. He was angry all of the time, except when he had too much to drink, then he wanted to get romantic, and I could not *stand* the thought.

And then it got worse. I felt as if I were drowning, and there was no one around to throw me a rope.

December 31, 1947

Dear Diary,

I'm flying! Jane is here! She popped in totally unannounced late Christmas afternoon. After last Christmas, when she wasn't able to be here, I thought I'd never see her on a Christmas again. She brought tons of exquisite things for Kate and me, handmade sweaters, yards and yards of the most beautiful hand loomed woolen material, jewelry, toys, adorable dresses for Kate, and more.

She didn't leave Tom out either, she brought him a lovely tan cashmere sweater and several fine handmade linen shirts. I could not believe my eyes when I opened the door and there she stood. Tom said later he thought I had been attacked I screamed so loud. She looks absolutely wonderful. We have been yakking non-stop ever since she got here. I didn't know how much I needed to talk. God, I missed her more than I can tell. And she missed me too. She tells me over and over how much she wanted to see my face and to hold "our Katie."

She is not happy with the way my life is going. Neither am I, but I'm not ready to give up yet. Tom's drinking is much worse, I can't deny that. Sometimes he doesn't even come home. Jane wants me to get a divorce. Right now, she says. I don't know what to do. Divorce is so final.

And what about Kate? She loves her daddy. She's too little to see or understand what's going on. I never had a father. I know how that feels. How can I deprive her of her father? Tomorrow starts a new year, maybe things will get better.

But, of course, they didn't. Tom was miserable. He came home late every night, drunk and angry. If there is anything worse than being crushed with loneliness in the same house with someone else I can't imagine what it is.

The only conversations we had were did you see my car keys, where are my shoes, drop off my shirts will you, and mostly, get off my back.

I began to find life with him intolerable, but still I hung on for Kate's sake. He usually came home so late she was already asleep, and all he ever saw of her was a tiny mound of blankets in her little bed.

At night, the stench of stale beer and cigarettes filled our room, and turned my stomach. I slept in a tight ball as far to the edge of the bed as I could get.

September 6, 1948

Dear Diary,

Today everything changed. My baby girl isn't a baby anymore. She started school and I have cried and cried ever since I dropped her off at her classroom door. I'm crying for happiness for her and the exciting new life she is about to begin and I'm crying for me because nothing will ever be the same again. I am going to see a lawyer about getting a divorce.

Tom is hopeless and I won't live like this any longer, not even for Kate's sake. Besides, she's beginning to notice that something is not right. "Are you sad, mama?" She asks me. "Are you going to cry today?" It breaks my heart. Jane calls me every week.

She has been so helpful through all this ugliness. God, I miss my Mum, I wish she was here to tell me what to do. If it wasn't for the baby, who stopped being a baby today (I have to remember), and my friend Jane, I don't know what I'd do.

The divorce was final on August 12, 1949. One day I was a married woman, and the very next day, it might have never happened. Five years, used up and tossed out.

Now that I look back on it, I can see that we never really had anything in common; he wanted to be free to hang out with his drinking buddies, and no responsibilities and I wanted the perfect home and the perfect husband I read about in ladies magazines.

That day I saw the lawyer, I came home early. Tom was there. He told me he'd been fired. Again. He was furious, said they had no reason to let him go. I cut him off in the middle, and told him that I had filed for a divorce. He looked at me, turned, and went upstairs. In a few minutes he came back down, with his suitcase. I asked him where he was going and he said, "Go to hell, Ida Mae." And he left.

April 30, 1953

Dear Diary,

It seems like a lifetime since I've taken a few minutes to catch up in here. Let me see, what has happened in the last five years. Five years! My God, time does fly even when you are not having fun!

I'm buying the print shop, that's the big news. Mr Berry is retiring and his son doesn't want to take over so I am. I am excited and scared. But I've worked there long enough to know what I'm doing. I think. I hope. I pray.

Jane has a nice part in a play off-Broadway. It's been running for ten weeks now and she is very pleased about that. She is working almost all the time, she even has an agent! How elegant can you get? The best news is that she is married. She called me last week to confess. And she's the one who swore she'd never let a man interfere with her career. I don't intend to let her forget it either!

Kate is doing very well at school, gets mostly A's and a smattering of B's. She's a much better student than her mother. She is a delightful little girl, happy-go-lucky and, like my dear Jane, very outgoing. I thank God every day for sending me such a wonderful child.

My life is mostly hard work and then more hard work, but I finally have gotten over the terrible sadness I felt for so long after Tom and I got divorced. What hurt the most is that he had wanted out for a long, long time. He had stopped loving me years before, if he ever loved me at all. I was such a fool.

I suppose Jane was right after all. It had nothing to do with me, just various body parts. Well, I won't do that again, I promise me.

May 28, 1954

Dear Diary,

Hah! Jane is divorced. Now we can be scandalous women together. She called last night in a fury. It seems her one true love was also the one true love of several other ladies. All at the same time.

Whatever happened to the Knights in Shining Armor we were promised? Poor old Aunt Germaine died last Thursday very suddenly. She died at home all alone, which is so sad. The medical report said heart failure. I think she just turned herself off. She had enough. The grocery delivery boy found her.

She had been unhappy for years, maybe even her whole life, and I am sure it's better that she is released from her pain at last.

Bernadette was at the funeral. I haven't seen her in several years and I hardly recognized her. She is much thinner but she does not look good at all. She had a terrible bruise under one eye which she says she got in a fall. I wonder. I asked her to come to tea next week and I hope she does, she looks like she could use a friend.

Jane refers to tea time at my house as the traveling tea party because I like to have it in different rooms depending on my mood, the weather, or whatever. She says you never know where you may find yourself sipping and nibbling.

It makes sense to me.

In the summer (before it gets too hot) I like to sit in the kitchen with all the windows and the back door wide open, where we can see and smell the beautiful roses in my garden. Mum planted some of them when I was a little girl, but many of the bushes have been there since the house was built.

I can close my eyes any time of the year and see the cascade of pink climbing roses spilling over the back fence, the pale yellow and the deep burgundy rose bushes almost breaking under the weight of blooms. When the weather is so dreary, in January and February, I comfort myself with the promise of soon, soon it will be spring, and the roses will be back.

In the worst of winter, curled up in the dark blue overstuffed chairs in front of the fireplace is the only place to be.

The sunroom has its own special charm, and I never know when I'll choose to be in there until I start to set the table, and that's where I find myself heading. I like it that way.

Once, on the afternoon of a raging spring thunderstorm, we took all the tea things upstairs to my bedroom. We lit half a dozen candles, piled up in the middle of my bed, and listened to the cold rain beat against the windows while we sat in a golden glow of perfect cozy comfort.

Now I must think about our last few days together. They must be wonderful. Something she can take with her wherever she is going. And something I can hold on to after she has gone and all I have left are a lifetime of memories.

Chapter Seven

As if there isn't enough on my plate. This day will go down in my memory book as a real doozie.

Kate took me aside this morning to ask me if I felt well, she has noticed that I'm awfully quiet. I suppose she means I'm not being my usual bossy self.

Sadness hangs in my bones like a chill I cannot escape. There is no relief. No warmth anywhere. I made some excuse about thinking I might have a touch of something or other, and after a strict admonition to get to the doctor at once, she let it go at that.

Then she dropped the bomb. She told me a rather nice-looking older man had been in the tearoom looking for me. He was an old high school classmate, she told me, and hadn't seen me in many years. He was in town on business and thought he might look me up.

My heart nearly stopped. Jane could have taken lessons from me at that moment, because I managed to act as if it as such fun, and I was ever so curious to see who on earth was here from out of my dark past.

I knew it was Tom. The last person I ever expected to see again in this lifetime. The last person I ever *wanted* to see again in this lifetime.

I left the tearoom feeling as if I was going to my own execution. Where could I go? I certainly didn't want to go home; Kate thought he might be there waiting for me. And that made me mad. It's my home. I'll not hide from anybody, much less Tom Tutweiler.

He was there. Sitting on the swing on my front porch, big and bold as you please. Looking very much the prosperous businessman. *Damn him.* I was surprised at the anger that welled up in me from nowhere. I had years ago gotten over any feelings I had about him, caring or anger, and yet here I was. Furious.

I drove in the driveway and parked the car. He stood up as I came up on the porch, holding out his hand and smiling, all warm and friendly.

"Ida Mae?"

He was still handsome, dressed in a pair of tan slacks, white shirt, and a blue and tan tweed sport coat. He didn't look like the boy I married at all, more like his father, and that made it easier. I took his hand, although I didn't want to, and said, "Hello, Tom."

I hated him. He had caused me more grief and pain than any young girl should ever have to go through, he abandoned our precious daughter, and yet here I was, holding his hand and smiling back at him. *Hello, Tom. You bastard.*

"I know this is a big surprise to you," he said, "but I was afraid if I called first you wouldn't let me come." *You got that right, Tom Tutweiler*. I opened the door and invited him in. I felt as though I was in some sort of surreal movie, and any moment the lights would come up and we'd all go home.

"Ida Mae, I had to see you. There's something I've needed to tell you for a long time now." I gestured him into the chair in front of the fireplace, and I sat in the other one. We stared at one another like strangers in a bus station.

I could see that he was nervous. He picked at his pants crease, and smoothed his hair. His eyes were as blue as ever, but the thick lashes were gone, and his curly blond hair was now thin and mostly gray.

He looked old. But then, so do I. The bright-faced, dark-haired girl that once was me went away a long time ago, and in her place is an old woman. Well groomed, but old all the same.

"Well, Tom, what brings you here?" I don't mean to sound tart, but the edge is there and I don't really care.

"Ida Mae, first let me say that Kate is so beautiful. It

really shook me up to see her."

Well, it should, you jerk. But instead I say, "Yes she is."

I almost tell him about Jenny, but then, why should I? He never cared enough to stay in touch with his only daughter, or is she his only daughter? So many thoughts are racing through my head I almost miss what he says next.

"Ida Mae, you know, I was an alcoholic when we were married. I didn't know that, and neither did you, but by the time I left here I was already in bad shape, and it got a whole lot worse from there on.

"Somehow or other, I have no idea how, I woke up in a hospital in Austin, Texas, recovering from the DT's. It was the worst damn thing. God! I was so sick I couldn't even walk, shaking like a leaf, and dying for another drink. It's absolutely crazy."

"Tom," I hold up my hands in protest, "do I have to hear this?" I don't want to know about his stupidity. I'm tired, and my best friend is dying and I don't feel like listening to his confession.

"Sorry," he says softly, "I'll get to the point. I've been sober for eight years now, and I go to AA meetings all the time. Those people saved my life when I didn't think I had a life worth saving." He stands up, and moves into the middle of the room.

I'm hungry, I can feel my stomach rumbling, and I want a cup of tea, but I'm damned if I'll offer tea to this man. I'd rather not ever have tea again. And my bra is killing me. All I want is to get out of these clothes.

"One of the things we learn to do in AA is to clean up the wreckage of the past. That means we have to go see all the people we caused harm to, and make amends. It's taken a lot of years to get up the courage to come back here, but I couldn't live with myself any longer. I want to make amends to you, for all the pain and heartbreak I caused you. I'm really, really sorry."

He comes over to my chair and takes my hand in his and

there are tears in his eyes. His deep voice is shaky, and there's no denying his sincerity. I am shocked. Tom, who would rather be chopped into little pieces than admit guilt for anything, apologizing? I pull my hand away. I don't want him to touch me.

"So, what do you want me to say? Oh, that's all right, Tom? I don't mind that you left us, that your drinking meant more to you than your wife and daughter? That you walked out of our lives without even a backward look?" I know that's not what he wanted to hear, but I haven't had eight years to get ready for this amends business.

He shakes his head, "No, of course not, I don't expect you to say anything. I just want you to know that I know I was terribly wrong, and I am truly sorry for all the hell I put you and Kate through. I don't expect you to forgive me. I was wrong, and I know it. That's all."

"So now what are your plans?" I'm terrified he thinks he's going to move back here and pick up his life as if nothing ever happened.

"That depends on you."

I knew it! I knew it! He wants to move back. I am one big wad of anger and discomfort. *Well, he's not.*

"How does it depend on me, Tom? Seems to me we've been divorced forever, and I hardly think that my opinion of what you should do with your life matters."

I notice that it is getting dark, and in the distance I can hear the rumble of the evening train. The horn blows the same mournful tune it's blown since I was a small child. The familiar sound soothes me, somehow. I can be nice. I don't need to be mean to this man anymore.

"I'm sorry, Tom, I guess you shocked me, showing up out of the blue like this. I appreciate your apology, I really do." There. I feel better already. But I still want my tea. I need my tea. I need to steady myself, like a ship that's been through a storm and comes out the other side, battered but still whole.

"Tom, would you like a cup of tea? I'm just about to make

some."

Oh well, so I caved in.

He smiles and shrugs. "Sounds good. I could use a little pick-me-up. I was scared to death you'd throw me out, or call the cops or something. I don't mind telling you, I put this off as long as I could, tried every way I could think of to avoid it, but it kept nagging at me."

Then I notice the ring on his left hand. A wedding band. "Are you married again, Tom?" So. He's not back here to try anything. That's a relief. My life is much too good just as it is. I have no intentions of trying to re-create long dead relationships. Let that particular dead dog stay that way. Forever.

"Yeah. I live in Houston." He smiles sheepishly, "I've been married six years. My wife, Carol, has two daughters of her own. That's what got me back here, as much as anything. I needed to make amends to you, and if you'll let me, I'd like to see Kate, and try to get to know her. Maybe even try to make up for the past a little. She may not want that, but I'd sure like to ask her. If she says no, well, I'll understand. I'll beat it out of here as fast as I can, and leave you alone."

"You already did that once, Tom Tutweiler." But I'm smiling as I say it. Suddenly, just as suddenly as it came, the anger is all gone. This stranger, sitting across from me at my kitchen table, might well be no more than just an old schoolmate, for all the feelings I have about it.

"I can't speak for Kate, but I think I need to be the one to tell her that you are here. I don't want her to be put on the spot. If she doesn't want to see you, it will be a lot easier for her to tell me no than it would be to tell you to your face. You understand?"

If my daughter chooses, she can have the father she never knew as a child. With all his imperfections and mistakes, and for however long it might take.

Kate never complained about her fatherless state, but when we talked about him over the years, sometimes I could see the sadness in her face. Her eyes glittering with unshed tears, or her little mouth quivering only so slightly.

Every girl needs a father, God knows I know that all too well.

I think if I had had a father, knew what to expect from a man, I might have made better choices of the men in my own life. Kate has already chosen her husband, but it's not too late to choose her father, too.

If he's the kind of man she wants her father to be, it would be great. And if he's not? Well, that's a bridge we'll cross if we need to.

We spend another hour in small talk. I tell him about the tearoom. He asks about Jane. I tell him she's fine, due in town in a few days. I cannot bring myself to tell him the truth. I simply cannot force the words out of my mouth.

He compliments me on how pretty the house looks. I thank him. I ask about his wife and her daughters, ask what is he doing now. He tells me he works for a large printing plant right outside Houston. He is happy, he says. Am I happy, he asks. Oh yes, I tell him, I am so pleased with Kate, and my darling granddaughter. We laugh about him being a grandfather; he says he's not old enough. I tell him, well, if you get to meet Kate you had better get used to the idea. I promise to tell Kate about him first thing in the morning.

And then he thanks me again for letting him make his amends and he leaves.

I am drained. So tired I wonder if I can even manage to drag myself up the stairs. But the promise of getting out of these clothes and into my good old almost antique robe gives me just enough energy.

Tomorrow will be a difficult day, at best. My heart goes out to my darling daughter. This is a moment we never planned for.

Chapter Eight

In the morning I call Kate. I ask her to stop by the house on the way to work.

"Mom, I think I knew it. Don't ask me how. I had this weird feeling the minute he walked in the door." She is standing in a corner of the kitchen, her slender arms wrapped around herself.

I want to hold her as I did when she was little. I do not want any pain for this most precious person in my life, and yet I know that I cannot save her from it.

She does not know much about her father. I answered her questions when she was young, as briefly as possible, no explanations, no lies, and no ugly stories.

I could have said much more, but that would have hurt her even more than it would have hurt him. She knew he had a problem with drinking, but I offered no gory details, and she never asked for any.

I explained that we were very, very young when we got married, and simply were too immature to make good decisions. She also knows I was pregnant with her before we were married. I never intended to tell her that part, but she found our marriage certificate stuffed away in my desk, and figured it out.

I told her it would not have mattered, we were engaged anyway, and all it did was move the date up by a few months. If she wanted to know more, she never let on, and I suppose I seemed reluctant to talk about it. For right or wrong, that was the truth. I did not want to talk about it because talking would have brought back memories I had no desire to recall.

She has decided to see him. I knew she would. I have given her his motel number, and she says she will call him today. I pray for her sake it works out well.

Now it's time to put all this aside, and focus on the moment.

I have an idea. If the weather will hold and I can pull it off. This time, my dear friend, I'm going to be the extravagant one.

And there's no telling what Bern, Kate, and Jenny have planned at the tearoom. They think we are celebrating a send-off for Jane before she leaves on a wonderful long-overdue vacation. Jane is adamant that we wait until the day before she leaves to tell them. She wants to have fun.

"I do not want the girls and Bern to sit there with long faces, mourning me before I'm good and gone. You know perfectly well it would be miserable, and I want to take our time together with me like a treasure I can enjoy."

"For what little time I've got left," hangs unsaid and unseen between us. The ghost of truth we will not allow.

She arrives this afternoon about four. Jane travels by train whenever possible. It's the only civilized way of getting where you mean to go, she says.

The truth is I think she's afraid of flying, but who am I to criticize? I'm the one who refused to go to Europe with her on the Queen Mary. I'm the one who has never even crossed the state line, nor am I likely to.

I'll meet her at the hotel, and we'll have dinner together. Tomorrow we'll have tea at Ladyfingers. Bern and the girls are preparing something special for her, I'm sure.

My heart is made of glass, and I must move with great care in order to keep it from shattering. These last few days must be our best; no time now for grieving. It will have to wait. I've got shopping to do, arrangements to make, and I've made it very clear to God what I expect from Him.

I've put in specific requests before, and on at least one occasion He answered me exactly as I wanted. I'm still not certain whether His answer was one of the best things that ever happened to me or the worst. Probably a little of both. That old saying "Be careful what you ask for, you may get it," rings all too true for me.

November 27, 1955

Dear Diary,

The most interesting thing has happened. Last month, Dave, the shop pressman for the past ten years, decided quite suddenly that he wants to retire. I was very upset to say the least. The only reason the shop has gone along as well as it has is because Dave is a rock. Nothing disturbs him.

I have been free to devote time to Kate after school simply because I never had to concern myself with how things were going at the shop in my absence. Old Dave could handle anything. I ran an ad in the paper but in this small town my chances of finding someone like him are not good to impossible.

So I prayed. Every night for a week I asked God to send me a good pressman. Right away. On this past Tuesday morning a clean-cut rather attractive young man came into the shop and asked me if I had run an ad for an experienced pressman. He just moved here a few days before and needs work. He's experienced and from what little I've seen, very good. I hired him on the spot.

His name is Robert Howe. I think my prayer has been answered!

I was so proud of my little shop. We were the only printer around for miles, and had all the business we could handle. The shop had been in existence for years before I bought it.

The customers were already there, and as far as they were concerned nothing changed. I had been taking care of them forever anyway.

I learned to love the oily smell of printers ink, and the chunka, chunka, chunka of the press putting out sheet after sheet of everything from the forms for the mayor's office to the birth announcements of the newest baby in town.

There's something very satisfying about taking blank pieces of paper and turning them into neatly stacked printed pages.

Sometimes, late at night I used to wander through the shop, admiring all the equipment that was mine. All the good and useful work that came about because of it, and how lucky I was to be a part of all this.

December 1, 1955

Dear Diary,

I'm in trouble again. I am attracted to Robert far more than I should be and I can't help it. What's worse, I don't even want to help it. When he stands beside me the warmth of his body drives me crazy. When he touches me, even for a second, I still feel it long after he's gone.

I am thirty years old and no man has ever affected me like this. When I'm alone he's all I can think about.

I've talked to Jane about it and she says I'm horny. Again. Or still. I don't know which. The problem is she may be right.

Robert and I work well together; the shop is going along as it always has. He is shorter than Tom, has dark brown hair and wonderful broad shoulders. He's not really handsome in the movie star sense, but he is rugged good-looking, I guess you could say.

When he smiles it starts in his eyes and lights up his whole face. I can't tell what he is thinking. He is always polite and friendly, but he must sense something. It's like electricity crackling and sparking between us.

I don't have the least idea of how to deal with this, but I know it's not a good idea at all for the business. I've always been a practical business person, I pride myself on that. Oh my God, how I want him to make love to me.

December 15, 1955

Dear Diary,

Ring all the bells! Bring up the band! Champagne for everyone! I finally had my first orgasm! Now I understand what they're talking about! It was glorious!

I called Jane first thing this morning and she was as happy for me as I am. Mercy, it felt good! I never could figure out why people made such a fuss over sex, but now I know!

Last night I had to go back to the shop after dinner to work on the books. I like to keep the billing current and it's easier when it's quiet. Robert was still there running a job that was due in the morning. See how reliable he is?

Anyway, we both finished up about nine-thirty and he asked me if I'd like to drop into Hannen's for a drink. I've never been to Hannen's in my life (or any other bar for that matter) and I decided it was time for a change. We had several drinks and a great conversation. It's amazing how much we think alike.

Before we knew it they were telling us to get out, it was closing time! I wasn't a bit tired and neither was Robert. Besides we weren't through talking so I invited him back to the house for a cup of coffee. I know now that he had been feeling the same attraction that I had. He told me that the first time he saw me he wanted to reach right over the desk, grab me, and kiss me. Isn't that romantic?

We were in the kitchen, I had my back to him making the coffee and he came up behind me and kissed me at the base of my neck. My whole body tingled. I turned around and the next thing I know we were kissing each other as if we had never experienced a kiss before, as if we could devour one another. I knew that we were going to make love. And it had to be right now.

We tip-toed into the downstairs guest bedroom. Kate sleeps upstairs next to my room, and even as badly as I wanted him, I had to think of her. Between kissing frantically and pulling each other's clothes off, we fell right over on the bed. I'm surprised it didn't break.

Then it began. His hands were everywhere on my body and where he touched me I was on fire. He kissed my breasts until I begged him to do it! Do it! He put himself into me, gently, slowly. Pushing in and pulling out until my body, on its own, moved in perfect rhythm with his. The divine dance of love. Warmer and sweeter than anything I had ever known before.

And then the explosion. Melting into the ecstasy of becoming one. Pulsing, pulsing, pulsing into the glorious oblivion of only feeling. Before early morning when he left, we made love twice more. I'll never be the same again.

Those silly mushy songs on the radio take on such personal meaning when you are newly in love. You know that they must have been written just for you. Everything shines with new intensity, new exotic color. Everything is laughable, you find yourself smiling for no good reason, and the world does indeed look rosy. No wonder we spend so much time and energy looking for the "right" one. I cannot think of another experience that comes even close to those beautiful feelings.

January 1, 1956

Dear Diary,

If life gets any better I don't know what I'll do. I am happier than I have ever dreamed of being. Robert and I are so in love. We touch and smile a hundred times a day. "I love you," he whispers in my ear or scribbles on a scrap of paper, dropping it on my desk while I am meeting with the mayor's assistant about printing the city budget plan for the coming year. "I love you," he prints in the paper dust back by the folding machine.

We make love every night and even sometimes in the afternoon before Kate gets home, because we just can't wait. We've made love in the darkroom at work, in the back yard, in the river at the park, and who knows where else we'll think of next. It is so wonderful.

All I have to do is look into those big brown eyes of his and I become jelly. Even writing about him like this makes me wriggle in my chair, remembering how he makes me feel.

And now, if this is not enough happiness, Jane is coming back to stay. She has been dating the director of the little theater for the past several years when she is in town and they have decided *they are in love too, and she is getting married on the 15th of this month! She is tired of the struggle in New York. She wants to be the big fish in the little pond, she says, and here is the place to do it.*

Life is good. No. Life is grand, and I thank God for all my wonderful blessings.

No matter what else has happened, I must say those first months with Robert were among the most glorious, and happiest, ever in my life. And even though things did not turn out the way I so ardently hoped they would, I'll always remember those sunny days with great pleasure. No regrets, either.

August 15, 1956

Dear Diary,

A little cloud has appeared. It's only a small one but I want it to go away. Robert told me a few months ago that he was still married. They had separated a year before he met me. He also married when he was very young and it was a big mistake. I can certainly understand that, I did the same thing.

The problem is, she won't agree to a divorce. I hate her. I love him so much but I don't like all this sneaking around. I want to be free to love him openly like Jane and her husband. He has asked me to be patient and, of course, I will be. What else can I do? I love him with all my heart.

Jane is our local star and she is basking in her new limelight. She really is a very good actress. I went to see her last night and I was amazed at how convincing she is. When she is up on the stage she is not my Jane at all. She is playing Blanche in A Streetcar Named Desire, and she actually becomes

Blanche. God, what a depressing play! I think I'd have to take to drink myself if I had to be that kind of person every night, even if it is only an act.

I am content with my act as it is right now.

It's too bad we can't "put up" those good times in our life, like plum jam, to take out later, when times are difficult. To open a jar of memories, and savor fully the sweetness of those truly happy moments. To taste clearly one more time the pleasures of the best parts of our life.

But we can't. At the most, we can only vaguely recall the feelings. I suppose that's for the best, because then we might also be able too clearly to recall painful times that are better left alone. Those years, however, were the plum jam years of my life

February 28, 1957

Dear Diary,

Bern came to tea this afternoon. She is now the manager of the Bon-Ton and doing very well. She really likes her work, and it shows. She looks better than I think I have ever seen her. Bern is a naturally big-boned girl, but she is solid and trim. Her hair, once her crowning glory, has gone quite gray and she wears it pulled back and clipped with a little black bow. It's almost glamorous. We had a good chat.

I must admit I have changed my opinion of her in the last few years. I think Aunt Germaine must have made her life very difficult and she reacted by being a brat only because she felt so awful about herself. She could never measure up no matter how hard she tried. How terrible to have a mother who can't be pleased and never approves of anything you do.

Thank God for my mum; I never doubted that she loved me with all her heart.

I've invited Bern again one day next week. After all, we are cousins and all there is left of our generation. She says very little about Billy. I have a feeling there is trouble but she won't talk about it.

Jane is doing famously at the theater. Definitely the toast of the (small but appreciative) town! Robert is my prince found at last. Kate is getting prettier by the day. She is very smart, bright as a new penny, as Mum would have said. I am so happy.

My plans are working quite well. I've spoken to the florist and I'm quite certain she thinks I've gone completely over the edge but she is ready and willing to do as I ask. I'll bet she has never had a sale come near what mine will be. It's kind of fun to surprise a few people around here. The mouse has come out of hiding at last!

Mr. Bennet at the hardware store has not only taken care of everything I need, but is going to send his stock boy to prepare for our arrival early in the afternoon of the day.

Now, nothing left to do but pray for good weather.

Chapter Nine

We arrive at Ladyfingers Tearoom exactly at four-thirty. As I had expected, Bern, Kate, and Jenny have been preparing to dazzle Jane. It works.

Our table has been set over to the far side of the main room where a bower of twisted grapevines and silk trees creates the illusion of a private park. The tablecloth and napkins are white silk moire, and the places are set with lovely white china service. A perfect yellow rose is laid across each plate, and on top of each rose stem, a pair of white crocheted lace gloves.

An exquisite antique tea set in brilliant yellow porcelain has been placed in the center of the table.

Hanging off the back of each chair is a charming white Milan straw wide-brimmed hat, replete with ribbons and bows and fabulous flowers in a rainbow of colors.After all, what lady ever went to tea without her hat and gloves?

A pair of two-tiered cake plates sit on a cherrywood Queen Anne tea cart placed beside the table. One cake plate holds tiny sandwiches garnished with the most delicately carved vegetable decorations I have ever seen, fragile yellow rose buds, some sort of miniature white flower, and sprays of tiny pale green leaves.

On the bottom tray, peeping out from behind a pile of sandwiches, lurks a perfect little mouse carved out of a radish. The other tray holds a luscious array of glistening dark chocolate petit-fours, lemon tarts, miniature napoleons, our trademark ladyfingers, and, of all things, white chocolate sea shells filled with dewy fresh red raspberries.

Where they got raspberries at this time of the year is beyond me.

They've definitely pulled out all the stops. The table is set for the four of us—Jane, Kate, Jenny, and me. I've asked Bern several times to join us, but she refuses. She will see Jane at dinner tomorrow, she assures me. Today she has to run the tearoom. Dear Bern, always thinking of others first.

Jane puts on an Oscar Award-winning performance. She emotes. She flings her arms skyward, as if in disbelief, she paces around the table, pointing out every wonderful sight, "Look at this, will you? Look at this setting! It's as beautiful as any Monet painting! And look at this food! How exquisite! How delectable!" She rants, she raves, she flails about. When Bern and the girls are flushed rosy with joy at their success, Jane finally settles down and we all sit.

Jane pours.

Kate's eyes sparkle, she is delighted that she has been able to please her beloved "Auntie Jane."

Kate and Jane have a special relationship. Jane was the one who took Kate shopping for school clothes after she got into junior high. They complained that my taste was too antiquated for today's woman, and so I was sent to the bookstore, or somewhere else out of their way, while they went on their annual spree.

Jane introduced Kate to the theater, museums and concerts. She taught her about a different world outside the bounds of Walton Falls. I've always been grateful for the way she expanded my daughter's horizons. And mine, too.

"A toast! A toast!" Kate demands.

My heart sinks. What kind of toast can we make, considering the occasion? Kate is ready to say something but before she can speak Jane lifts her cup.

"To mothers and daughters, to wives and sisters, to women everywhere, and to best friends forever!"

We touch our cups together.

"Hear, hear," we murmur.

There is no place for dreariness at the table. We soak up the elegance and charm and return it to the room embellished with laughter.

September 30, 1957

Dear Diary,

Every day when Kate comes home from school we share a few minutes over a cup of tea. She tells me about her day and I tell her about mine. At least most of it. I suppose the same is true of her.

And I remember once again how much I enjoyed tea with my mother. Times change but I am happy that they don't change altogether. It's a nice tradition I share with my Kate.

There's some not so happy news, too. Jane had tea with us today and she told us that she is going back to New York. She misses the excitement and challenge of the "Big Apple" as she calls it. I'm not sure what that is going to do to her marriage. She says they'll deal with it as it comes but I have a feeling that she is going to get away from her husband as much as she is going to a life she prefers. We shall see.

I will miss her terribly. It has been wonderful to have her at my fingertips these last few years and now I'll have to adjust again. I want my best friend to be happy and if New York is what it takes, I'll deal with it.

Robert is nowhere nearer to a divorce than he was the day we met. I love him passionately. He is a delight to be with and we have so much fun together. Still, I have to admit I can't help but feel frustrated and even a little bit angry at the everlasting delays, delays, delays.

Kate has pulled me aside to whisper in my ear.

"I called him." She is smiling, but I can see her dark eyes begin to tear. She fights for control, then smiles at me. My brave little girl. "We are having him over for dinner tonight. I feel so weird, Mom, I don't know even what to call him. "Dad" sounds so strange. It's hard to say."

"Then don't." I put my arm around her, "Don't call him anything. Be your sweet, charming self and don't worry about it. You've had lots of conversations where you haven't mentioned the person's name, and never gave it a second thought. Later on, you can decide what you want to call him. Or *if* you want to call him."

She looks at me with that almost sideways glance, "Mom? Is this hard for you? I'd rather not have anything to do with him if it's going to hurt you even the teeniest bit."

She sniffs, "I feel so guilty. Like I'm being disloyal, or something." I shake my head in protest, "No, my darling girl, don't worry about that. You need to have a relationship with your father if you possibly can. It's not going to have any effect on you and me. We have a lifetime together, and you can't change that."

She hugs me briefly, and flashes me that same dear smile she had the very first day she walked into school, *I'm being brave aren't I Mama? I'm not scared, am I?*

Underneath, there's a small piece of me that feels more than a little weird too.

This man has popped in on me and my daughter after all these years, like a king coming back to claim his throne after the queen has spent her lifetime trying to take care of the kingdom. *Hey, I'm back. Get out of my chair, I'm here to take over again. Sorry to be gone so long, but you know how it is. A guy gets busy.*

Now, I must tell Jane. That ought to be fun.

April 15, 1958

Dear Diary,

I was right. Jane is getting divorced. She says she is thinking of setting up a part-time sideline practice as a divorce counselor. There are plenty of marriage counselors out there, she says, but damn few have the expertise she has about getting divorced. I asked her if she would take on Robert as her first client... he sure could use some help.

I think we're done. He shows no interest in changing the status quo and I have no interest in maintaining it. How very sad for both of us. He will always be my prince. Even after it turns out his armor is quite badly tarnished and dented, I'll never stop loving him. So there, I've gone and done it again. Fallen in love with someone who can't love me back. I wonder why.

That's one of the big differences between Jane and me. She does not seem to mind as much when a relationship disappears. She seems to be able to don and doff husbands like I don and doff my underwear. On a regular basis. I have no heart left to break and no heart to do this to myself again.

June 27, 1960

Dear Diary,

She did it again. The woman has no sense. Jane has married the leading man in a television soap opera she has a regular part in. He's fifteen years younger than she is, for God's sake, and looks like a teen-ager. She brought him for a visit, showing him off like a new puppy that followed her home by accident. She says, why stop now when she's on a roll?

She has a great new part as the villain mother-

in-law, a part she has had plenty of exposure to during her adult life. Or at least what passes for adulthood. I think she never got past sixteen, myself. Oh well, that's my Jane. Kate is in love too. It must be the weather or something. I intend to stay inside and keep my umbrella up even indoors just to be on the safe side.

Kate's love is a very nice young man of whom I have reluctantly approved. I am a little unhappy about the fact that he is five years older than she is but she is very mature for her age, she has never found boys her own age all that interesting. His name is Jimmy DiAmato. He seems to be a nice enough young man. She is not even seventeen yet, with so many choices still ahead of her. I am hoping this will pass. God knows I do not want her to make the same painful mistakes I made.

Kate is very sensible and Jane has offered her a fully paid education at the school of her choice which she is quite excited about. Then this young romance will end or go on hold. My guess is it will end. The less pressure I put on her, the less likely she is to do something foolish.

August 2, 1960

Dear Diary,

Bernadette came to tea today and I am very upset about what I am convinced is happening to her. She has a broken arm which she insists she got when she slipped on her front steps. Every time she comes to visit she is wearing a bruise or a cut or an injury someplace on her body. She says she is naturally clumsy but I don't believe her for a minute.

I know how violent and bad tempered Billy has

become, everyone talks about it, and I hear stories at the shop about the brawls he gets into. I am very worried about her. Bern is a sweet, good woman who has never gotten the love or understanding she needed in her whole life. I can't believe now that I once disliked her so intensely. There isn't a mean bone in her body.

I have tried and tried to get her to tell me what is going on and to assure her that she can come to me if she ever needs help. It's like talking to the doorstop; she changes the subject every time. Well, she knows I am here and when the time comes I'll welcome her with open arms.

October 12, 1960

Dear Diary,

I am thinking of selling the print shop. I have had a very good offer from Mr Berry's grandson and I believe I am going to take it. I have an idea of what I'd like to do next but I haven't yet said a word to anyone. There's a part of old downtown that dates back to at least 1850 and a few smart people are thinking of restoring the main street to its original elegance, opening gift and antique shops, that sort of thing.

I think I'd like to get the place that was once the restaurant and turn it into a Victorian tearoom. A place for other mothers and daughters to enjoy what I have learned to treasure in my life. I even have a name picked out. I'll call it Ladyfingers, after the cookies Kate liked so much as a child.

By the time we get back to the house, it's dark. I enjoy winter, but I have to admit by the end of February I am ready for it to be over. I begin to get impatient for longer days.

Jane and I plop into the two well-worn dark blue chairs in the living room, I turn on the little gas burner in the fireplace, and we sit there staring into the dancing orange and blue flames. Not much to say. The day has been grand and we don't want to spoil it by words used simply as mortar to fill in the silence.

Tonight is not the night to tell her about Tom. This is our time together, and I'll not have it marred.

"I used to regret that I chose to avoid what you have." Jane's voice is so soft I can barely hear it above the hissing of the grate. "I never stood still long enough to have a family or a real home. By the time I realized what I had missed out on, it was too late."

She can't see me smiling, but she can hear it in my voice. "I always wished that I could be more like you, out in the big middle of life, seeing and doing things I never dared. You were my window on a world I was far too timid to visit by myself."

"Aren't we a pair? You do your thing, I do my thing, and between us we've done everything!" Jane chuckles gently.

I have to agree. Between us we have done everything. What a great thought.

Chapter Ten

"Why, Jane, why?" I have to know, to try to understand.

"I don't really know. I suppose I've become my mother. You know, the perfectionist thing? I couldn't bear the thought of being anything less than perfect. And then, when I finally admitted to myself that this was not going to go away it was too late, I was furious. At her, for making me this way. And at me, for being stupid. But it wasn't her fault at all, it was mine. Now I can't go back and choose again, so I'll go gracefully. Isn't that just perfect?"

She tosses her head, and makes a pretend bow in her chair.

I have to laugh. What a woman.

Tomorrow is my special day for us and the next night the girls are coming to dinner. That's when we'll break the news to them. God, I dread it. Then she leaves.

"Well, I am feeling terribly unhappy about it. You are going off and leaving me again, only this time I know you won't be back with big bunches of flowers. How am I supposed to manage without your calls and your never-ending advice, which I rarely take anyway?"

"You'll manage," she replies dryly. "You are far stronger than you realize. Look at what you've done with your life. You've built two businesses with no help from anyone. The print shop earned you a good living for a long time and provided the money for the tearoom. And you know how successful that's been! You've raised a wonderful talented daughter, given her a set of values and her own sense of self that have produced an even more wonderful grandchild."

"You've rescued Bern from what could have been a death sentence, and you were kind to a selfish, wicked old lady who lied about her marmalade. If you'll lie about marmalade, you'll most likely lie about anything."

She smiles, and brushes an errant hair out of her eyes.

"And besides all that, you have turned out to be a damn fine woman yourself. Course, I helped with that part," she concludes, sounding smug.

"Jane, let me go with you."

I don't know where that came from. I certainly hadn't planned to say it. Having blurted it out though, I find I mean it.

"Are you serious? After all these years you'd actually go away with me?"

"Yes, I will." My insides are quaking, but I am serious. If she'll let me go, I'll pack this minute.

"No, my dearest friend, I can't let you go. I must have elephant genes somewhere in my lineage or something like that. Going off into the woods to die, away from the herd, y'know. This is the one journey I truly, truly prefer to take alone. Don't ask me why because I don't really know, and I don't feel any compulsion to figure it out. I will say though, it pleases me that you love me that much, because I know how you feel about travel!"

June 23, 1962

Dear Diary,

Ladyfingers Tearoom is a fact. I signed the papers yesterday. Scary. Kate is ecstatic; she absolutely bubbles with plans. I have not seen so much enthusiasm from her since she left for school. I am afraid she is not as happy away as I had hoped she would be. She calls me almost hourly with some new idea. And I must say, they are excellent, very unusual ideas which I plan on using.

We are committed to an antique theme in keeping with the rest of the restoration on the street and Kate wants to start shopping for antique hats and feather boas for our guests to dress up in while they are having tea. We'll hang them all over the walls in the front room where the guests will wait till we seat them. Part of the fun will be picking out the right hat to wear and maybe even a swishy feather thing. I think it's a delightful idea and so does Jane. She promised to start shopping in the back streets of New York, in the old junk and second-hand stores right away. She says there's a motherlode of that sort of stuff hidden away in those places.

There's tons of work to do, scrubbing away years of dirt first, then painting, papering, buying all the tables and chairs, and everything, everything we need. I'll have help I didn't expect but am mighty glad to get.

What I have long suspected has happened. Bern has admitted that Billy has been beating her up for years. There's good news though; she has finally had enough, and left him. She showed up on my doorstep last night, weeping, she told me she feared for her life. I welcomed her with open arms

She will live with me for a while until she can find her own place. I've asked her if she would like to help me with the tearoom and she said yes. So that is settled. I'm very relieved that the awful life she has lived is over. Maybe now, after all these years, she can find some happiness. I hope so.

September 20, 1962

Dear Diary,

The tearoom opened today. It was a smashing success. The mayor's wife, Mrs Harold Hunniker, cut the ribbon and everyone who was anyone at all was there in their best bib and tucker. It was magnificent, marvelous, wonderful, and glorious. If I do say so myself.

Jane came in from New York and all the ladies were nearly overcome with excitement. She has become quite famous as a result of her part in "My Children's Lives" as the bad-tempered, scheming mother-in-law. I could not be more pleased at the way the tearoom turned out.

Jane and Kate cornered the market on hats of every style and color imaginable. They look wonderful hung on Victorian style hooks, over gilded mirrors, and piled high on two huge ornate credenzas. The guests had a hilarious time, trying on dozens of hats to find the right one, and the feather boas were great fun!

The main room is lovely. We have placed groupings of silk trees and big pots of silk flowers here and there. It gives one the feeling of being in a Victorian garden. Each table has a different tea set on it, another one of Kate's ideas.

The biggest hit of all were the six child-sized tables and chairs placed in a bower of trees for our very young lady guests. Toy-sized china tea sets on pink tablecloths looked absolutely charming. The little ones loved it!

Bern and Kate had on Victorian maid outfits with white lace-trimmed aprons and matching puffy caps. They carried around big trays of tea sandwiches and trays of pastries and sweets. It was simply great and we are all giddy with exhaustion and triumph.

November 3, 1962

Dear Diary,

What a day! Bern came into her own today in no

uncertain terms. She has told me about what a living hell her life had been with Billy. He abused her horribly, the monster! He told her she was ugly and stupid and that no one in their right mind would have her so she had better do everything exactly the way he told her to or he'd throw her out to starve. He beat her all the time.

Once he even came up behind her and for no reason that she could figure out, he attacked her, beating her almost unconscious! What a beast! The really awful part is she never knew why he did it and didn't dare ask for fear he'd do it again.

Well, last night she changed all that. We were cleaning up in the kitchen at the tearoom, and without even a knock Billy came crashing in through the back door. It was obvious that he was roaring drunk. Billy never was a very big man, but he had gotten quite fat over the years, and he has a loud raspy voice.

I was terrified, but Bern just stood there without flinching. She had the strangest look on her face, sort of solid, unmoving. Billy swore at her and told her she had better get her fat ugly ass back to the trailer or he'd teach her a lesson she would never forget.

Bern reached over and picked up our biggest cast-iron skillet off the stove and held it in front of her like she was about to swat a big bug. "C'mon ahead then, Billy," she said, in a flat sort of voice.

I was frozen, too afraid to move.

Billy stopped and stared at her for the longest time, then he told her she was a useless old hag anyway, and not worth having, and he spit on my clean floor! Then he turned around and sort of swaggered towards the door slowly.

Bern let him go about two steps, then she yelled

at the top of her lungs, "Yah!" and slammed that big old skillet down full force on the top of the stove! Billy shot three feet straight up and ten feet straight out that door in one jet-propelled move. It was wonderful!

Bern and I laughed so hard our faces hurt and we danced around the kitchen like two loonies! I can't wait to tell Jane the next time she calls. So much for that miserable bully.

June 15, 1963

Dear Diary,

The one thing I did not want to happen has gone ahead and happened in spite of me. Kate is going to marry to Jimmy. She came home a few weeks ago and brought all her things home with her. I knew the minute I saw her pull up in front of the house with the packed car, and him in tow, that for my Kate, school was over.

She wants to stay home, marry her prince (and he is a prince, I have to admit), and work at the tearoom. She promises she will complete her degree here at home. I caved in because to do otherwise would be useless anyway. Kate is very clear on what she wants for her life and I respect that.

So now I must prepare for another wedding. I do hope it is less dramatic than mine was. I can do without the brawling and bleeding that made mine such an event.

Was that real? It seems almost like a movie I saw years ago and have forgotten all but the highlights. Or lowlights, actually.

Jane will be back in town next week and she will be a great help in planning the wedding. She will be here for a month. I am so pleased. She is getting yet another divorce. I'll bet her lawyer would have to make a big adjustment in his way of living if Jane ever stopped getting married and divorced.

Do I care? Not a bit! Do I love her just as she is? Yes, dear diary, yes.

August 17, 1963

Dear Diary,

Today my precious only daughter was married. Once again, it was a small wedding, only family and a few very close friends. But this time it was perfect.

Kate looked gorgeous in a simple ivory silk dress. She wore her dark hair pulled up in a tumble of curls and had little creamy white roses and baby's breath tucked in here and there. I wore a soft pale green chiffon thing that I will probably never have on my back again, but it did look nice.

Jane wore a deep rose silk suit, with delicate crystal bead trim and she looked smashing. So elegant. Next to Kate, she was the center of attention. Being the big New York star and all.

Jimmy's family is Italian, and of course, they made a huge fuss, with tears and hugs and kisses all around. It was great fun. I must admit, I'm happy to have Kate back, I missed her more than I would have thought. And at long last, I've had the wedding I always wanted.

We have decided to take tea upstairs in my bedroom as we did once before so long ago. It's gloomy outside and dreary and the warm glow of lamps and candles makes the room seem welcoming and cozy. We make a nest on my bed. Jane props herself up in a pile of pillows against the headboard and I curl up near the foot against my down comforter.

"Jane, do you remember when we were kids? You picked me up like a poor little starving sparrow and fed me crumbs of friendship and kindness when no one else even noticed me. Why did you do that? I've always wondered."

"Because I liked you." She grins at me and her eyes twinkle, "It's as simple as that. I didn't care about what the other kids were doing. I saw you, and I liked you. I wanted you to be my best friend from the first time we were in our homeroom class. You looked, I don't know, like you were more in control of yourself. More than the rest of the kids, and far more in control than I felt in myself."

"Good God, I was scared to death! What you took for control was really abject terror!" We laugh at how full of fears and worries we were in those days (always unspoken), and at how little we knew of what real fears and worries were skulking around the corners of our lives yet to come.

"You're not scared now?"

She looks serious, considering the question, and after a short silence she answers, "No. Not now. I was for a while, terribly scared, but not anymore. I think, although I've missed some things, like having a child and some stability in my life, on the whole it's been a grand adventure. There are always trade-offs. You can have this, but then you cannot also have that. I have deliberately chosen not to grieve over what I do not have but to enjoy and celebrate what I do have. What else is there to do?"

Yes. What else, of course. Then she puts the question to me, "How about you?"

"Nothing to be everlastingly sorry for. I've made some foolish mistakes and some choices that turned out to be less than wise for me, but on the whole, now that I think about it. …my life has been quite good. I've had the love affair that many women only dream about, and even if it didn't turn out like the fairy stories promised, it was still fun while it lasted. My child and my grandchild are the joy of my life. My business is hard work, but it's also great fun. And through all the times, good, bad, and indifferent, I've had one thing I could always count on. My best friend. You."

We smile at each other, and hold hands across the bed tray where we've put our cups.

"Jane, there's something I've got to tell you. Tom's back." I can see the storm rising. She sits straight up and crosses her arms angrily. I soothe her, patting her arm as is she was a child in distress. "It's okay. He came back to make amends to me for all the grief he caused. Apparently it's part of something they have to do in Alcoholics Anonymous. He's been sober for the last eight years"

"Well, he damn well ought to be sorry. I'm surprised he had the nerve to show his face around here. What does he want now, call everything even and move back in?"

"No. He's remarried. He just came back to do this amends thing, and of course, he wants to see Kate."

"Kate! The nerve of that man, how dare he—"

She jumps up so quickly the teacups rattle in their saucers. Before we have tea all over my bed I grab her hand, stopping her in mid sentence. "Wait! I felt the same way, but if Kate wants to see him, I have got to support her choice. I can't prevent her from having a relationship with her father, even if you and I think he's a day late and a dollar short. He seems to be genuinely sorry for his behavior, and if she wants to get to know him, I'm all for it."

She looks at me like I've gone out of my mind.

"Well, maybe not *all* for it, but what can I do? I'll smile and be happy for her. I am happy for her. Besides, I can't keep dragging the past along behind me, it's too heavy."

She smiles again and sits back down on the bed. And suddenly I notice how thin her hands are, the dark circles under her eyes, the little cough that never stops. My friend is dying. I can't refuse to see it anymore. And there's one more question I must ask.

"Jane, how am I to know?"

"I've already arranged for that. Don't worry, darling."

The tea and my heart have both gone cold. It's time to go downstairs again.

Chapter Eleven

It's the moment of truth. The weather is perfect, cold and clear. Fresh snow fell last night, covering everything in a blanket of white that sparkles in the sunlight.

I've checked with the florist. She sees no hitches at all. Mr Bennet assures me that all will go exactly as planned. Good. Ida Mae Tutweiler's traveling tea party is about to take on new meaning.

I pick up Jane at the hotel at three. It's early for a proper tea, but it's dark by five these days, so we'll push it a bit. I've warned Jane to dress warmly and she has taken my advice to heart. She's bundled clear up to the top of her head.

"You look like Nanook of the North."

"Well, you said dress warm, so I did! What kind of a devious plan have you got up your sleeve, woman?" I hum to myself and ignore her question. We drive right past my street, and out of the corner of my eye, I can see Jane staring at me curiously. I am delighted that I have her wondering. I intend to keep her that way as long as possible.

When we get to the park I can see the gazebo in the distance. Pale pink and glittering silver ribbons flutter in the breeze but Jane hasn't noticed them yet. We pull up in the parking lot, and I can see that a narrow path has been shoveled from the lot to the gazebo steps.

So far, so good.

Jane has discovered the decorations. The ribbons and greenery entwining the outside posts have turned the gazebo into a giant wedding cake. I take the wicker picnic basket from the trunk, and grab her hand. "Come on, missy, it's teatime!"

As we go up the three steps into the gazebo I can see that

it is even prettier inside than I imagined. All around the walls bright red, pink, and deep purple tulips are massed with sunshine yellow daffodils, pale blue hyacinths, and huge pink peonies (where on earth did the florist get peonies?). The table is set with Mum's pink tablecloth and the white porcelain cabbage tea service.

It is as warm as toast. Mr Bennet's electric heaters are doing a great job. Thank goodness the city fathers saw fit to put electricity into the gazebo last year. The record player, hidden away behind a screen of greenery, is playing lively baroque music.

I unload the basket, spread the table with a plate of still-warm scones and a cut-glass jelly dish of my birthday marmalade. We are ready for a springtime tea.

Outside the gazebo snow begins to fall. Big fat, lazy flakes silently drifting down.

God certainly knows how to help set a scene.

"Ida Mae, you are the most wonderful person in the whole wide world!" Tears are running down her cheeks but she is laughing, too. "Only you would think up such a grand scheme! Oh, this is glorious! Come here and give me a hug!"

We stand for a long few minutes holding each other tightly. There's nothing to say, but there's nothing that needs to be said. We know everything we need to know without any words.

"Sit, madam, and enjoy!" I command her.

Jane swoops elegantly to the table, and arranges herself gracefully on the wrought-iron bench beside it. She is being ever so glamorous. I have to laugh at her high drama.

"You know, Ida Mae, I've been thinking. You and I, and all the women like us, are the last tattered remnants of the Victorian Age. When we are all gone it will be the end of an era. We're as doomed as the dinosaurs!" Her voice is deep and dramatic.

She strikes a pose like a statue of mourning. Her head hung down and one hand half covering her eyes, one long leg stretched out in front of her, the epitome of grief. If she had wings they'd be drooping.

"Jane! Where on earth did you get that idea?"

"Listen. Think about it. Our mothers were raised by women who grew up right smack in the middle of Victorian times. And all of their values, morals and beliefs were passed on from mother to daughter without much change. Oh, sure, each generation modified them some, but the underlying structure remained very much the same as it always had. Until our daughters were born. Then the big changes started really showing up. So, there you have it. We are the Last Of The Victorians." She wipes an imaginary tear from her eye.

I can't stop giggling. Jane has a way of milking even the grocery list for all it's worth.

"And to think I never gave it a thought! Nor, I suppose, has much of anyone else. And I further suspect, if I ran about reminding the general populace of the impending loss, they might applaud instead of weeping. We were a pretty stuffy bunch anyway!" I pull my handkerchief from my purse, and delicately blot my eyes, too.

"There! You see! You've proved my point." She points at me, "Who carries clean pressed handkerchiefs these days? Certainly not anyone under sixty that I know of. You can't even buy a decent hanky anymore. But have you ever been without one? I don't think so. Would you carry one of those nasty little packages of paper thingys instead?

"Never!"

"I rest my case, madam!"

We laugh at her silliness, and at the sheer beauty of the day. Tomorrow we'll cry. Today is for fun.

We stay until there's almost no light. Jane helps me pack up the tea things, the leftover scones are crumbled, and scattered for the birds. The flowers have served their purpose, they are left for the pleasure (and wonderment) of whoever passes by.

We return to the house and to the comfort of fat, soft

chairs and a cozy fire.

I remember when I got those chairs. I was twenty-seven and they were the first new pieces of furniture I ever bought. I was so excited, something new in a house full of old things—things that were old when Mum was a bride.

I had no idea then of the value of old things. Old furniture, old clothes, to me were a sign of poverty, not treasure. I have come to realize over the years the things I value most are the things I have had the longest.

I have a navy blue turtleneck sweater, I don't even remember where or when I got it, but I pull it out every winter and look forward to the first cold day when I can snuggle into it. Winter wouldn't be the same without my good old sweater.

Old friends are that way, too. Sometimes we begin to pay too much attention to the worn spots and the lumpy places and forget about the warmth and comfort that only a well-worn friendship can bring to our lives. That was true of Jane and me. There was a time when we set aside our friendship because the lumpy places got in the way and we forgot about the value of our love for each other.

February 25, 1965

Dear Diary,

My darling Kate has given birth to a magnificent little girl. I am ecstatic. They have named her Jenny, after Jimmy's mother, which is fine with me, my name is too old fashioned for today's child.

If there is anything grander than having your own grandchild laid in your arms for the first time I cannot imagine what it would be.

Kate and Jimmy are a wonderful pair, they will be excellent parents, I feel sure. It is a joy to see how much they care for one another.

Jane has gotten married again. I cannot understand why she keeps on doing this, one right after the other. It's like she keeps on buying a toy and as soon as it stops working right or turns out to be not as advertised, she throws it away.

It's none of my concern but it does bother me all the same. She has won some sort of award for her acting in daytime TV. Good for her! Except for this ridiculous tendency to get married at the drop of a hat, I'm very proud of her.

February 2, 1967

Dear Diary,

Well, she's done it again. Jane has gotten yet another divorce. Now she is pressuring me to take a trip with her. She wants to go to London on the Queen Mary and has offered to pay all my expenses. All I have to do is go. The problem is I don't want to.

Although it's true I have never left town I don't think it's because of some ridiculous problem, it's just that I have everything I need right here, so why go hopping all over the place when I'm happy where I am?

I don't want to leave Kate and my precious Jenny. I didn't have my mother when my child was young and I know how much I missed her. I don't want to do that to Kate even for a little while.

Jane refuses to understand how I feel and she says I am letting her down when she needs me. Well, I don't think so, I think she is being very selfish in her demands.

We had a very unpleasant argument on the phone last night and I'm afraid our friendship has taken a turn for the worse. I hate that, but she can be quite self-centered sometimes, and there's nothing I can do about it.

March 29, 1968

Dear Diary,

I miss Jane. I feel as though an important part of my life is gone and I am very sad about it. I miss her visits and the hours and hours on the phone. I am so sorry I refused to go on the trip with her. I've thought and thought about it and I see now that the truth is, I was afraid. I was afraid to go away from the familiar, the usual. Why, I have no idea. Now it's too late. She is angry with me, and I know Jane, she's divorced me too. For the first time in years, I feel lonely again.

Jane sighs, "Do you remember the time when we had that fight over you going to London with me?"

I am startled by her question, "How strange… that's exactly what I was thinking about!"

"How did you feel while I was away? Did you miss me?"

"Of course I missed you, silly! Don't you remember?"

"Well, I am going away again but I'll bet it's not for good this time either."

"What on earth do you mean?"

"Do you believe in an afterlife, like heaven or something?"

"Um, I think so, yes, I believe I do. Yes, I definitely do, as a matter of fact."

"It's going to be interesting," she murmurs. "I'm looking forward to it. Who knows, we may well be sitting around having tea in another dimension, or another place, or another life, again sometime. Who's to say this is all there is?"

Who indeed?

Chapter Twelve

Jane comes to the house about four. Tonight is dinner with the girls. I have forced myself all day to keep my mind on the moment I am in, I can't even allow myself to think half an hour ahead; it's too scary and painful.

"Well, long nap, madam?" I inquire. I'm trying to keep things light, for her sake. And mine too, if I have to be honest about it.

She makes a pouty face, "Sorry, I had some last-minute stuff to attend to. I hate lawyers. They always try to make things so bloody complicated. God knows, I've spent enough money with them, I ought to know that by now. Kate gets everything. Not that it's all that much. The junk has already been pitched."

She looks tired and ill. Her beautiful eyes are sunken deeply into her head, and her face is gaunt and drawn. She drops into one of the kitchen table chairs like a sack of groceries. Not like her at all.

"Jane, we can call off tonight if you want. We can do something else if you are not up to this."

"No, no, don't be silly. Just give me a minute to get my breath, and I'll be fine. I doubt if I'd ever have a moment's peace if I left without saying goodbye. You'd probably end up with the tearoom haunted. A poor ghost who can't go to her heavenly reward until she makes her proper farewells."

"Hmm-mm-mm. A haunted tearoom. I like that. Could you do it? That way I'd know you were still around even if I did stick my hands right through you every time I tried to give you a hug."

Jane laughs. "I'll ask when I get to wherever it is I'm going. You'd probably see a real jump in business. Especially around Halloween." I'm puttering around the kitchen. It's toasty warm and familiar smells of dinner cooking fill the room.

I've prepared Mock Duck, a favorite of mine since my childhood days. Mum used to make it for Sunday dinner, and I'm sure her mother made it for her when she was little. God knows how far back the recipe goes. Centuries, I'd be willing to bet.

With it I'll serve creamy scalloped potatoes, made from scratch, thank you very much. No mixes or boxes of pre-made, pre-cooked, pre-fab food for my family and friends. There'll be golden coins of carrots glazed with a spoonful of orange juice, brown sugar and butter, finished off with tiny spirals of grated orange peel. Delicious.

For dessert I've made a sweet apple pie, topped off with my own special cinnamon ice cream. Jane loves my cooking.

You are the world's greatest cook, she has always said. *And I am close to the world's greatest actress. So you cook and I'll always act like I'm enjoying every bite.*

And she does, too. But I don't think she is acting.

Kate and Jenny arrive at six, full of tales about the day's adventures at the tearoom. Bern is half an hour behind them. She would no more leave Ladyfingers before the last chore is done than she would go for a walk down Main Street in her undies.

I send them all to the living room while I put the finishing touches on the meal.

Kate corners me in the kitchen. She looks concerned, frowning, "Mom? What's the matter with Jane? She looks terrible. Haven't you noticed?"

"Yes, darling, I have. She's not well. We'll talk about it after dinner, okay? Hand me that covered vegetable dish, will you?" Kate hands me the dish. She obviously wants to talk more, and I just as obviously am not going to.

The oldest ceremony in the history of the human race is sitting down to eat a meal together. Ever since Og and Ogette made a place in their cave to share a stone bowl of mastodon soup, we've been gathering around a table of some sort. Whether it's to celebrate, to mourn, or to just plain enjoy nourishment, eating together has always been an important event in the day. I suppose the ceremony of tea came about exactly for the same reasons. We need to be together, to nourish our hearts and our minds along with our bodies.

We are together here at this table, for the last time, and it's all I can do to keep the tears locked in my throat, not pouring out all over my plate.

It's a quiet meal. Pleasant enough, but the usual bantering, laughter, and waving of silverware is mostly absent. There's tension in room, and we glance at one another, asking questions with our eyes. *What's the matter? What's happening here?*

Dessert is nibbled at, and coffee cups refilled.

"Jane?" Kate breaks the silence. "Are you sick?"

"Yes." Jane speaks so softly I can hardly hear her. "Yes, I'm very sick. And I'm sorry to say, it looks like I am about to be finished."

No one speaks. No one moves. The tears I have kept at bay all evening spill over. No one even notices. They are all staring at my dear friend.

"No!" Kate shouts. "No! That can't be!" Her face is contorted, her fist pounds the table. "Oh my God. No!" She bursts into tears. "Aunt Jane," she wails.

Jenny is white as a ghost, her napkin clutched against her open mouth, her blue eyes huge and round, glittering with tears. "Aunt Jane, are you sure? Have you had a second opinion…?" She asks in a quavering voice.

"Yes darling, I'm sure. I've had second and third opinions even. It's time for me to leave."

Bern has pushed away from the table, standing, tears streaming down her cheeks, wringing her strong hands like an old washerwoman. Jane stands too, and holds out her arms. She is crying. The girls rush to her, and for a few minutes only the heartbreaking sounds of women weeping fill the room.

Somehow, we all get into the living room. Jane is seated on the couch with Kate and Bern close on either side and Jenny crumpled at her feet. I go for the Kleenex, hand the box to Jenny and pull up the old Queen Anne side chair. That chair has always been around, and I'm glad of it tonight. I need the security of my old treasures.

"Mom?" Kate turns her tear-streaked face to me, "You've known this, haven't you?" I nod, unable to speak. She reaches for me, puts her hand on my knee. "Mom, why didn't you tell us? You shouldn't have kept us in the dark like this."

Jane speaks gently, "I made her keep it a secret. It's all my fault. I didn't want to spend my last time with you being sad, don't you see? I wanted for all of us to have happy memories, I wanted my days to be filled with your smiles, not your tears. So you can blame me. I'm the villain." Jane blows her nose violently and Jenny giggles, then starts to cry again, quietly. She puts her arms around Jane's legs and cuddles up against her. "I love you, Aunt Jane. I don't want you to leave me." She says through her tears.

Jane brushes Jenny's long blond hair back softly, "I know that, my dear heart, I don't want to leave either, but I'm afraid I've not been given any choice in the matter."

Kate rests her head softly on Jane's shoulder. She sighs deeply, the raggedy wavering sigh of a child who has cried too hard. Jane kisses her tenderly. "I never had a baby of my own. But I didn't need one, because I had you. A big part of my happiness was because of you. Never forget that." Kate is too devastated to speak. She nods, stroking Jane's arm and hand, then she brings Jane's bony hand to her lips and kisses it.

Bern's face is as red as a beet. She cannot stop crying. Jane pulls an arm free and puts it around Bern, pulling her close. "You are going to have to step in here, Bern.

Somebody has got to see to it that these girls toe the line. I'm passing the baton to you."

Bern nods, and hugs Jane back. "I got it," she whispers. "I got it."

Jane tells them her plans, and after they all express their strong objections, she firmly tells them the same thing she told me.

"It's written in stone." She will have her way and we must accept it.

At ten o'clock Jane shoos them out the door. No one says goodbye.

"Take care," they say. "Be careful," they say. "I love you," they say over and over. But no good-byes. That final word is never mentioned.

Jane leaves right after them.

"I'm so tired, dear friend, I hate to leave you with all the mess, but I just don't think I have another two minutes left."

Once again, my house is empty. All I have are a stack of unwashed dishes, the remains of an apple pie, and melted ice cream.

I wish tonight would never be over. I'd be happy to stay here, doing the dishes and cleaning up forever if it meant tomorrow wouldn't come.

Chapter Thirteen

"Mother!" Kate is laying down the law to me. I'm Mom when things are on an even keel. When she starts with the Mother thing, I am usually in trouble or I'm about to be instructed about some slippage in my life.

This time she surprises me. I'm not being instructed, I am being invited. She is prepared with a long list of reasons and explanations of why I should accept. She wants me to spend time with her, before it's my turn to go away, although that is certainly not mentioned.

I surprise (and amaze) her right back. I wave away the list and accept her invitation. Jane will never believe it.

She leaves today. I have not allowed reality to interfere with our time these past few days. Now I can no longer ignore it.

She will be here at two o'clock and she will leave at four sharp. She will not let me take her to the train station. She says this house is where we should say goodbye, this is where we have shared our lives, not in some grubby public building.

I've got a good stout pot of Earl Grey ready to go. She'll need it and so will I.

The cab is here. Jane comes flying up the sidewalk, unbuttoned coat billowing in the freezing winter wind. I run out to meet her. I have to admonish her to button up, she'll catch a cold running around like that.

"Really? I've already caught more than that, silly. Who cares if I get a little old cold?"

"You will, if you have to depart this vale of tears in a wild fit of sneezing! It wouldn't be dignified."

We are being flip, and I don't want to be. There are

things, important things, I want to say, but the words stick in my throat. I tuck her arm in mine and lead her into the house. Perhaps in a few minutes I'll be better able to talk.

God, give me the courage to accept the things I cannot change.

"Ida Mae?"

"Yes?"

"There's no need to say anything. Not by this time. Everything we've ever needed to say has already been said a dozen times and if we could speak a foreign language, I'm sure we'd have said it in that, too."

"Well, I've never said I was sorry I wouldn't go to London with you. And I should have gone."

"That's true. But I know you. You've worn that hair shirt long enough. Take it off and pitch it, do you hear me?"

I pretend I'm struggling to pull off a shirt that fits too tight. I wriggle out of it, holding it out in front of me like something very smelly, open the front door, and throw it away.

June 1, 1970

Dear Diary,

The most wonderful thing has happened! My best friend has come back! I thought I'd never see her again and it made me so sad for so long I forgot how to feel any other way. Underneath where no one could see was an empty place that only she could fill. But now she's back and I am happy! Happy! Happy!

I was sitting at the kitchen table last night, reading the paper and relaxing, when I heard someone at the front door. I had not yet unlocked it from when I got home and couldn't see from the kitchen who it was. As soon as I stepped into the hall I saw her! She was waving a silly little white flag and had a huge armload of beautiful red roses for me!

Glory be! My best friend forever is my best friend forever again!

One last time we begin the familiar ceremony. Cups are filled with steaming amber tea. Plates of buttered scones await the finishing slather of jam. We are quiet. Soaking up the beloved comfort of one another.

"Jane? I have to tell you something."

"Tell."

"I'm going on a trip."

"I don't believe you."

"It's true. Kate and Jenny are going up to the Maine seacoast for a month this summer, Jimmy will come up on weekends, and I am going with them. It's time to unlock the doors I've placed around myself."

Jane is staring at me, slack-jawed. "My God, it's a miracle!"

"Well, maybe a small one at that." I can't help but give her an only slightly foolish grin.

I think the best part of growing older is how much easier life becomes. The events, needs, and demands we perceived as vital to our survival in early years take on far less urgency. Most of them, if not yet achieved, really don't matter all that much anymore. Many of them are completely forgotten.

What begins to matter a great deal is who you love and who loves you. Jane has been such a one to me. Not the only one, of course. But the first, besides my Mum. I think because of her unwavering love I learned that I was loveable in a world in which, for whatever reasons, I often felt shunned.

Jane has been a vital part of my life. How can I tell her that before she leaves for new adventures I cannot share?

"Ida Mae?"

"Yes?"

"When you are in Maine? When you see the seagulls swooping over the waves, think of me. I'll be happy and free just like they are. You be happy for me."

I hear the cab honking out front and I realize he's been honking for several minutes now. It's time for her to leave.

She stands up, swallows the last of her tea, and holds out her arms to me. We embrace, both crying silently, then she turns and half runs out the front door.

Just before she steps into the cab, she turns, waves, and blows me a kiss.

Chapter Fourteen

She's gone, I tell myself over and over. She's gone.

And once again, as I have so often been in my life, I am alone in my house. But this time it's different. There is emptiness in these rooms that I have never felt before. They are too big, too cold, too hollow. I feel frozen in time. Waiting and waiting. For what, I do not know. For the message I don't want to hear. Don't want to know.

How can I believe that Jane will never call again, never knock on my front door, then burst through in a swirl of laughter and love? How can I? One minute she is here and the next she is not. And all I have is her word that I will never see her again.

"Wait! Wait!" I want to shout, "I haven't said goodbye yet!"

I can't cry. There are no tears left to shed.

Kate and Bern and Jenny wander in and out of my days in a silent haze. Specters at an invisible grave. I know I must attend to them, they suffer as much as I do, but I have nothing to give.

We sit together now and then, at tea, deriving what little comfort we can from each other's company, but the truth is we are each wrapped too tightly in our own private pain. We have to be together, but there is nothing to say.

This will pass. I know that. And I want to tell them that, but they wouldn't believe me anyway, and all the platitudes in the world, heaped high enough to fill these sad rooms to the ceilings will not bring them one faster moment of peace. They'll know when they know.

When, I wonder, will I?

The days are long, like the late winter weather. The

pewter gray skies, flat and dull, suit my mood. I don't think I could bear sunshine right now.

I find myself watching every medical report on TV, hoping to hear the news about a great breakthrough in the cure of cancer so I can call her and tell her where to go to get well. I scour the newspapers for articles to clip and send to her. But there is no address. No phone. The connection has been cut completely.

She's gone.

The days, the weeks, the months drag on, like dark misshapen beads strung one after the other on a waxed string. Each one the same, each one marking… what? The end? The beginning?

And there lies the truth. I still want to believe she will come back to me. Somehow… I'll wake up one morning and there she'll be… standing on my front porch.

"Surprise!" she'll shout, "I'm well!"

I dream about that moment. Plan for that moment. Hope desperately for that moment.

"Oh for heaven's sake!"

I can hear her.

"Get a grip! It's over. O! V! E! R! You can't change reality. I don't care how hard you wish." She'd be annoyed to no end with me. I know that. As frivolous as she was in many ways, she was a die-hard practical realist in many others.

Kate is worried about me, I can see it in her eyes. Hear it in her voice. She calls or stops by every day. Brings me some exotic new tea, a plate of little cookies from Bern.

She fusses over me like a mother hen, and I want to shoo her away. I want to be left alone to mourn, to wail and rend my garments like the women in the Bible.

Jane laughs. I really *can* hear her. "Talk about your high drama!" And I have to smile, too.

I loved her. She will always be my best friend. Outside, the ice is thawing. I can hear the drip of melting icicles plopping onto the snow heaped against the house.

The Last Chapter

It's finally spring again. The tree branches are outlined in that fragile shade of new green I love so much. Under the trees, through patches of old snow and last year's debris, daffodils are beginning to show.

I've set tea in the sunroom. It's a fine day, full of the wonderful promise of life. New, glorious life. My favorite time of the year.

Today is a tea alone day. A day of putting out the dreary winter cold and letting in the happiness of beginning again. I've used Mum's pink cloth. A small plate of radish sandwiches and hot-from-the-oven scones await my pleasure. A wisp of steam curls from my beautiful teapot. A perfect day.

The doorbell rings, and even now, my heart stops for a second. I wish it could be Jane, standing there with an armload of roses and that silly white flag once again. Telling me that there was a miraculous cure, and she is back to be with me for a long time yet. I know better, but still, I hope.

Through the glass I see a UPS woman holding a brown cardboard box. I sign for it, examining the box for clues of its contents. There are none, and the return address is meaningless to me.

Well then, open it, and see what's come to surprise me on this perfect day.

Inside the box, wrapped in layers and layers of crisp white tissue paper is an exquisite frosted crystal seagull skimming gracefully over a sparkling crystal wave.

The message I never wanted is here.

I hope I see her again someday. I have to believe I will.

I put the crystal seagull on the table in front of me and together we have tea.

Ida Mae's Favorite Recipes

Mum's Recipe for Scones

¼ cup soft butter
1-3/4 cups all-purpose flour
2-1/4 teaspoons double-acting baking powder
2 eggs
1 tablespoon sugar
1/3 cup heavy cream
pinch of salt

Place the butter, flour, baking powder, sugar, and salt in a bowl, and blend with knives or a pastry blender until chopped into small pieces the size of a pea.

Then beat the eggs, take out two tablespoons of the beaten egg and set aside, add the heavy cream to the remaining beaten egg, and mix well.

Pour the egg and cream mixture into the dry mixture, and quickly blend together. Mum always said not to overdo this step, or the scones will not be fluffy.

Drop by heaping tablespoons on a cookie sheet, brush a few drops of the reserved egg on the top with your fingertips, and sprinkle with a few grains of sugar. Demerara is best.

Bake in preheated oven at 450 degrees for about 15 minutes. This recipe makes about 12 delicious scones. Sometimes, just for a change, I'll add a teaspoon or so of sugar and a good stiff dash of cinnamon and nutmeg to the dry mix. Probably not proper according to all the rules of good scone making, but I do it anyway. Serve with butter and your favorite jellies or jams.

Tea Sandwiches at Home

Take thin sliced white, wheat, or wheat-berry bread and trim all the crusts. Throw the crusts out for the birds. (Waste not, want not, Mum used to say.) Using a cookie cutter or a small glass, cut one or two rounds out of each slice. Spread each round with *one* of the following:

Softened butter
Softened cream cheese (can be mixed with a small amount of chopped fresh chives or parsley)

Top one bread round with a thin slice of peeled cucumber, or several thin slices of radish. Place another round on top. Very simple, but ever so nice with a good cup of tea late in the afternoon.

Tea Sandwiches from Ladyfingers

At the tearoom we try to be a little more elegant. On the trays we pass, along with the simple home tea sandwiches, you will find a selection of the following:

CREAM CHEESE & OLIVE ROUNDS

Use one 8 ounce package of cream cheese and about 40 small pimento stuffed olives (chopped) for 20 little sandwiches.

Use a firm white bread, and cut into 40 rounds with a cookie cutter or a small glass. Soften cream cheese with a spoonful or so of the brine the olives are packed in, mix in the chopped olives and spread on white bread. Put another round on top.

If you want to get really fancy, spread a thin layer of plain cream cheese (softened with the olive brine) on the top slice of bread, and place a pimento stuffed olive slice on it with a tiny parsley leaf off to one side.

SHRIMP PATE ROLL-UPS

Trim the crusts from 32 thin slices of firm white bread, and flatten them slightly with a rolling pin. Spread each slice with *Shrimp Pate* (see below), then roll it up tightly. Place the rolls seam side down right up against one another on a cookie sheet. Cover with plastic wrap and top with a damp towel; chill overnight. Before serving, tuck a small sprig of parsley or watercress in the ends. Watercress is best.

Shrimp Pate:

> Chop fine or mash 2 cups small cooked shrimp,and mix with ½ cup soft butter and ¼ cup mayonnaise. Add a pinch of salt, chopped fresh or dried dill, and a dash of cayenne. Mix and blend until almost smooth. You can also use crabmeat instead of shrimp, or even a mixture of both.

SMOKED SALMON TRIANGLES

Soften cream cheese, and mix with a little squeeze of lemon and fresh minced dill. Cut thin sliced rye bread into triangles, and spread with mixture. Top each triangle with a small piece of thin sliced dry smoked salmon, the very best you can find.

Even if it's $20 to $30 a *pound,* the few wafer-thin slices you will buy won't cost but $2 or $3 at most and the difference in taste is well worth it. Garnish with a tiny triangle cut out of a black olive. I'd tell you to use truffles, but I *know* at $300 a pound, you're not likely to, so do the black olive thing instead.

CHICKEN & PISTACHIO TEA LOAF

Please read this whole recipe before you begin, to be certain you have everything on hand. Save yourself a last-minute mad dash to the store.

Chicken salad filling

1 cup finely diced cooked chicken breast
¼ cup salad dressing
¼ cup finely chopped celery
pinch of salt
dash cayenne
optional: a dash or two of curry powder
Mix ingredients well, and chill.

Pistachio Filling

1-1/2 cups pistachios, shelled (of course)
1-1/2 tablespoons salad oil
1 cup soft butter

Whiz the pistachios in a blender, adding oil as needed to make it smooth. In a small bowl mix the nut mixture and the butter until well blended. Chill. It will separate easily, and you will need to soften and blend again before using.

Putting it all together

1 loaf white bread and 1 loaf wheat bread, unsliced

Trim all the crusts off both loaves of bread, then, carefully cut each loaf in four slices *longways,* so that you can stack four of them (two white and two wheat) together to make a whole loaf. Double this recipe if you want to make two loaves, or freeze the leftover slices for later use. Spread the bottom white piece with the chicken salad, top with a wheat piece, and spread with the pistachio spread. Top with another piece of the white bread and spread with more chicken salad. Top all that with one more slice of the wheat bread.

Frosting for Tea Loaf

3 8 oz. packages of cream cheese
3 to 4 tablespoons milk
dash of cayenne
pinch of salt
1-1/2 cups pistachios, chopped fine

Whip cream cheese and milk, adding milk a little at a time, till of spreading consistency. Add cayenne and salt, blend in, and set aside, but do not chill. Chill loaf several hours, tightly wrapped in plastic wrap. Then frost loaf top and sides. Press chopped pistachios all over top and sides of loaf. Chill again at least several hours, then cut into slices, using a bread knife and a gentle sawing motion.

HAM & ASPARAGUS ROLL-UPS

Thin sliced white bread, crusts trimmed (With this recipe, you decide how many you want to make)
Thin slices of ham
Fresh blanched asparagus spears
Soft butter or mayonnaise

This is best made in the spring, when the first fresh asparagus comes on the market. Snap the woody base of the asparagus off, and save for asparagus soup.

Bring a large pan of water to a full rolling boil, and add the asparagus. Allow to cook only long enough to be tender-crisp. It is only a matter of a few seconds to a minute or two, depending on how thick the asparagus stalk is. You just have to keep fishing a stalk out, run it under cold water, and taste. When it is right (still almost crunchy) quickly pour the water and stalks into a large strainer. There's nothing better than asparagus when it's cooked right, and nothing worse when it's overcooked!

Immediately run cold water over the stalks to stop the cooking process. Try not to eat it all before you go to the next step. Flatten the bread slightly with a rolling pin, spread with a small amount of butter or mayo, place a slice of ham on the bread, trimming it to fit. Place a stalk of asparagus on one end letting the tip stick out, and roll the whole thing up. Place seam side down, fitting them tight against one another. Cover with plastic wrap, chill several hours, and serve.

Sweet Treats for the Tea Table

LADYFINGERS

Kate's favorite, and our signature cookie.

1/3 cup cake flour

Sift before measuring, then spoon lightly into measuring cup. After you have sifted and measured, sift twice more. (Don't ask me why, Mum always said the flour had to be really light for the ladyfingers to be delicate. So we always sift. And the ladyfingers are always perfect.)

1/3 cup confectioners sugar, sifted before measuring and set aside in a separate large bowl
1 whole egg
2 egg yolks, set the whites aside in another small bowl

Beat the egg and yolks until *very* thick and creamy. This takes time, but it is a very important step.

Whip the reserved egg whites until they are stiff, but not dry. Gradually beat the confectioners sugar into the egg whites, and beat again until it is thick and stiff, then gently fold in the egg yolk mixture and add

¼ teaspoon real vanilla… not the imitation stuff, it's nasty.

Then… gently fold in the flour. Spoon the batter into a paper cone, and spritz out on an ungreased cookie sheet, or use a decorator tube to make them fancy. *OR*... drop by half teaspoons on the cookie sheet. Bake in preheated oven at 375 degrees for about 12 minutes. Makes 30 elegant little cookies.

DEL CAIN'S COOKIES

This is a longtime family favorite recipe of a most favorite neighbor. It's so good we use it at the tearoom, and everyone loves these fudgy little morsels.

1 stick of butter, melted in a heavy saucepan.
When butter is melted add:
2 cups granulated sugar
½ cup milk
½ cup cocoa
1 teaspoon vanilla
optional: ½ teaspoon ground cinnamon

Bring to a full rolling boil, then allow to boil, stirring constantly, until it reaches "soft ball" stage. If you don't have a candy thermometer, you can drop a dab of the mixture into ice cold water; if it can be picked up and rolled into a soft little ball, it's done. It only takes about three minutes to get to soft ball stage. As soon as it is ready, dump in the following:

2 cups uncooked oatmeal
1 cup chopped nuts (pecans are best, I think)

Mix together, and working quickly, drop by spoonfuls onto wax paper. Let the little cookies cool, and try not to eat them all in one sitting. Makes about 60 cookies.

PECAN LACY COOKIES

Another favorite of mine. Deliciously crisp and sweet… and easy to make.

2 eggs, beaten till foamy and light

Then add:

1-1/3 cups firmly packed brown sugar
Beat till well mixed, then add:
5 tablespoons all-purpose flour
1/8 teaspoon salt
1/8 teaspoon double-acting baking powder
1 teaspoon real vanilla

Mix thoroughly, and add:

1 cup chopped nuts (pecans or walnuts)

Grease and dust with flour two cookie sheets. Drop batter by half-teaspoon well apart; these spread quite a bit. Bake about 8 minutes in 375 degree oven. Makes about 50 wonderful cookies. Might as well make a double batch. They are that good.

LEMON SQUARES

We serve these instead of tarts, because they are much easier to make, and delicious! They are the perfect touch with a cup of good Earl Grey.

Preheat the oven to 350 degrees. Line a 10 X 15 jelly roll pan, or a cookie sheet with sides, with foil. Use the heavy duty stuff, so you can lift it out of the pan later. Lightly grease the foil.

Crust

2 cups all-purpose flour
½ cup confectioners sugar
1 cup softened butter
½ teaspoon vanilla extract

In a mixing bowl, combine all of the above, and blend using a pastry blender, or process in a food processor, using the metal knife blade. When it is crumbly, pat it out evenly in the prepared pan. Bake at 350 degrees for 20 minutes.

Filling

While the crust is baking, prepare the following:

4 eggs
2 cups granulated sugar
6 tablespoons flour
¼ teaspoon baking powder
6 tablespoons freshly squeezed lemon juice (use only fresh; bottled stuff just doesn't taste nearly as good)

1 tablespoon grated lemon peel (use the fine side of your cheese grater and grate the yellow part only, not the white stuff)
½ cup whipping cream

Beat the eggs till blended, add the rest of the ingredients and mix well. Pour the filling over the prebaked crust while it is still warm, and return to the oven. Bake for 25 minutes more. Cool, then sift a little confectioners sugar over the top.

When the pan is completely cool, lift out by the foil liner, and cut the dessert into squares. If you want to be extra elegant, just before serving top with a fresh raspberry and a leaf of mint, or a small strawberry, sliced and spread into a fan shape. This is one of my favorites.

TINY CREAM PUFFS

These tasty morsels are made with cream puff paste, or more properly *Pate A Choux*. The French invented this wonderful treat many, many years ago, and I think we should call it by its proper name. Besides, it will really impress your friends and guests. They are so simple to make, and yet many cooks shy away because they think they are too complicated. Nothing could be further from the truth, but you don't have to tell everything you know. Let 'em think you are a talented gourmet cook.

Use a heavy 1-½ or 2 quart saucepan.

1 cup water
6 tablespoons (¾ of a stick) of real butter (no substitutes here), cut into pieces
1 teaspoon sugar
pinch of salt
pinch of nutmeg
1 cup sifted all-purpose flour
4 eggs, at room temperature (very important)

For the glaze:

2 egg yolks, beaten, with ½ teaspoon water.

Bring water and butter to a boil; as soon as butter has melted remove from the heat. Immediately dump in all the flour, and beat vigorously with a wooden spoon until it is thoroughly blended.

Return to high heat and stir constantly till the mixture

leaves the sides of the pan and begins to form a film on the bottom of the pan.

Again, remove from the heat, and still in the pan, make a well in the center of the mixture with the wooden spoon, and break one egg into it. Beat until the egg is thoroughly blended. It will look funny, and "separate" into little pieces for a minute, but just keep on beating; it will all blend together soon. Then add another egg, beating it in thoroughly. It goes all funny each time, but smoothes out. Repeat until all four eggs have been added, one at a time. Be sure the mixture is well blended and smooth. That's all there is to it.

For tiny puffs, drop by rounded teaspoon on a buttered baking sheet, about 2 inches apart. Brush the tops of the puffs with a glaze of beaten egg yolk. You can use a small pastry brush or your fingertips. After all, if fingers are good enough for the great Julia Child, they are certainly good enough for the likes of us!

Bake in a preheated oven at 425 degrees for about 20 minutes. The puffs are done when they are double in size, golden brown, and firm and crusty to the touch. Remove from the oven, and pierce with a small sharp knife to let the steam out.

Turn off the oven. Then set the puffs, still on the cookie sheets, back in the turned off oven, leaving the door ajar, for about 10 more minutes. Then remove and cool on a rack. Makes about 36 small puffs.

You can make larger puffs easily. Just use larger mounds of puff pastry on the buttered cookie sheets. Bake at 425 degrees for 20 minutes or until the puffs have doubled in size and are lightly brown. Then reduce heat to 375 degrees for 10 to 15 more minutes, until they are firm and crusty to the touch. Remove from the oven, cut a one-inch slit in each one, and return to the hot, turned-off oven, leaving the door ajar, for another 10 minutes. Large cream puffs will be somewhat uncooked in the center; you have to cut them in half, scoop out the damp centers, and allow them to cool and crisp in the oven before you reassemble them.

You can leave out the sugar and add a little more salt and a dash of pepper, for a main dish puff. Fill with creamed chicken for a favorite that has been around for centuries.

Filling for cream puffs:

Whipped cream is wonderful, of course, or you can use the following recipe. Since you have gotten elegant with the *Pate A Choux*, you might as well fill it with the equally elegant *Creme Patissiere*. (That's vanilla custard, but in French it sounds so much more glamorous I wouldn't think of calling it anything else.)

1 cup granulated sugar
5 egg yolks
Beat the egg yolks and sugar together until mixture is pale yellow, and looks thick and sticky.
Beat in:
2/3 cup sifted all-purpose flour

Then add:

2 cups of milk brought just to a boil (Be careful, don't let it boil over!)

Remove from heat and add the egg mixture to the hot milk very slowly. Use a wire whisk for this step as it works best. (If you don't have a wire whisk, you really should get one; they are very handy. Get a good quality one, with a round metal handle, not the wire-handled kind; it's much easier to whip and seems to be more effective with less effort.)

Place the mixture back over medium high heat, and stir rapidly with the whisk. As the custard begins to thicken it may be a little lumpy, but it will smooth out as it continues to cook. After it reaches a boil, reduce the heat and simmer, stirring constantly, for two or three minutes. Watch the heat, as custard tends to scorch rather easily. After it is thick, remove from the heat and add:

1 tablespoon butter
1-½ tablespoons vanilla

OR:
2 teaspoons vanilla
3 tablespoons instant coffee

OR:
2 teaspoons vanilla
3 ounces semisweet baking chocolate, melted in:
2 tablespoons coffee

A dash of cinnamon is wonderful in any of these, as well.

Creme Patissiere will keep for a week in the refrigerator. Smooth a little melted butter over the top to keep a skin from forming. It may also be frozen.

To assemble the Cream Puffs

Fill the bottom half of each puff with a spoonful or so of the custard, put the top on, and drizzle *with Glacage Au Chocolat* (Chocolate Glaze.) Serve on a gold paper lace doily… delicious and impressive. This is another dessert that looks beautiful with a strawberry fan, a mint leaf, and a couple of green grapes for a garnish. How elegant can you gct?

Glacage Au Chocolat

2 ounces semi-sweet baking chocolate (the very

best you can find)
2 tablespoons coffee, (the flavored coffees, such as hazelnut, work well for this recipe, too)

Place in a small metal or glass bowl, place the bowl in a saucepan over very hot but not boiling water, and stir until the chocolate has melted into a smooth cream. Remove from the heat and beat in:

6 tablespoons unsalted butter, cut in small pieces

Place the bowl in a larger bowl of cold water, and beat until somewhat cool. While it is still warm enough to pour, spoon over the cream puffs.

These are just a few of our best recipes. I hope you enjoy them, and when you are sitting with your best friend over a pleasant afternoon cup of tea, have a sip and a nibble for all of us at Ladyfingers.

Ida Mae's Favorite Dinner

After going through all the description and details of my dinner party, I could not leave you without including those recipes as well. By the way, these really are from my childhood.

I have no idea why Mock Duck is called that, but my guess is that many years ago, probably in England or Ireland (because that's where my mother's family was from), when poor people could not afford duck they used a stuffed flank instead, and called it *Mock Duck* to make everybody feel better.

Even the great MFK Fisher in her wonderful book *The Art of Eating* lists the recipe but offers no explanation. We are free to use our imagination.

And *my* imagination pictures a family sort of like Tiny Tim's from Dickens *A Christmas Carol* all sitting around the seventeenth-century rough wood slab table saying, "Wot's ter eat then, Mum?" and she replies in her most cheerful voice, "Well, I've got a surprise fer yez tonight! It's your favorite! *Mock Duck*!" Of course, since she was so happy about it, they had to pretend to be, too.

When you prepare this dish, then, give a thought to all the people who've enjoyed it in the centuries before us.

MOCK DUCK

two medium-sized flank steaks, *butterflied*, (will serve six with leftovers)

three cans beef stock
1 box dressing mix, chicken flavor is best
1 ball white string, to tie the rolled-up meat

To butterfly means to cut open long ways to open like a book. You can ask your butcher to do it for you, but tell him that you are going to be stuffing it, so he should be careful not to cut holes in it. He probably will anyway, but you can repair them by opening up the steak and slicing (flat ways) off small "patches" to cover the holes. The dressing will hold them in place. The flank should be cut all the way to the other edge, to open like a book, but keep it in one piece.

Prepare the dressing mix according to package directions. I'd tell you how to make homemade dressing, but if you don't already know how, you most likely don't want to (it's a lot of work for not all that much better results), and the box stuff is perfectly good.

Pat the dressing out over the flank steaks, to within about 1/2 inch of the edge, then roll it up gently. Don't try to roll it so tight that you smoosh the dressing out. After it's rolled up, tie it tightly with the string I told you to get. Be sure to tie the ends as tightly as possible, to keep the dressing inside the roll. Some will leak out anyway during the cooking process.

After you have finished both rolls, heat a large deep skillet with ¼ cup of vegetable or olive oil. Brown the flank steak rolls on all sides and then remove from the skillet. Transfer the meat to a roaster and add two of the cans of beef stock to the pan.

Roast, covered, for about 3 hours at 350 degrees. Keep an eye on the level of liquid and add the last can of beef stock if needed. When done, remove the rolls from the stock, and set aside in a warm place, covered with a clean tea towel. The roasts should rest for about twenty minutes to firm up a bit.

To make gravy, use 4 tablespoons of flour mixed thoroughly in 1/2 cup cold water; slowly stir into the simmering pan juices. Any dressing that has escaped will blend right in

To serve, cut the string and slice the rolls into 1-inch (or slightly more) slices. Cold leftovers can be sliced thin, and make great sandwiches.

Scalloped Potatoes

Another dish we can thank the French for. Only they call it *Gratin Dauphinois*. Call it whatever you like, it's an excellent side dish. However, mashed potatoes go well with Mock Duck if you haven't got the time for this recipe. Preheat the oven to 425 degrees.

To serve eight you'll need:

Two pounds of potatoes (the regular brown ones) peeled, sliced, and placed in cold water (To keep them from turning brown, that's why.)
A fat clove of garlic, peeled and cut in half
4 tablespoons butter
1 teaspoon salt
1 teaspoon chili powder (optional, but it adds a very special spark, you'll be surprised!)
1 cup grated Swiss cheese
1 cup whole milk brought to a boil (Be careful, it can boil over in a flash. Do not allow yourself to get distracted. It's a mess to clean up. I ought to know, I've done it often enough.)

Rub the garlic clove all over the inside of a 10" x 2" deep oven proof casserole dish, then grease with one tablespoon of the butter. Drain the potatoes, and dry them on paper towels. Spread half the potatoes over the bottom of the dish, sprinkle over half the cheese, half the salt mixture, and half the remaining butter. Layer the rest of the potatoes over, and repeat the process with the remaining cheese, salt mixture and butter. Pour over the boiling milk and pop in the oven, uncovered. It will take 30 to 40 minutes to bake. They are done when the top is nicely browned, and a knife slips in easily. These will keep warm at the back of the stove for a good half an hour.

ORANGE GLAZED CARROTS

Here's where fresh counts. Frozen carrots just can't compare to the real thing. Canned carrots are a disgrace. In my humble opinion.

To serve eight:

16 medium to small carrots
½ stick butter
½ cup orange juice + one tablespoon
1 tablespoon light brown sugar + 1 more tablespoon
1 teaspoon fresh grated orange rind + a little of the rind cut into teeny slivers for garnish

Peel and slice the carrots in rounds, about 1/3" thick. Place carrots in a medium saucepan, add ½ cup orange juice, 1 tablespoon of sugar, and barely cover with water. Cover and cook until carrots are not quite tender. Drain and add the rest of the orange juice, the rest of the brown sugar, the butter, the orange peel, and the slivers of peel. Simmer until the liquid is syrupy. How could anything this good be bad for you?

APPLE PIE AND CINNAMON ICE CREAM

And now for the deepest, darkest secret of my life. First you go the grocery store and you surreptitiously buy the very best frozen apple pie you can find. Don't let anybody see you. Then go buy a box of *Demerara,* or *raw sugar*. Then sidle over to the frozen desserts section and buy a gallon of the very best quality French vanilla ice cream. If you don't have any ground cinnamon at home, get that too. If you really want to keep your secret, slip the frozen pie into a nice pie pan.

The day before you plan to serve the pie, put the frozen ice cream in a large bowl and let it soften. When it is all melted around the edges mix it all together until it is like soft frozen yogurt (the kind we love on a hot summer afternoon.). Add about 6 tablespoons of cinnamon and blend well. Pour the ice cream back into its container and refreeze. It's yummy over all sorts of pies. And it's especially great with hot fudge sauce, when that's exactly what you need.

Before you bake the pie according to directions, brush the top with milk. Go ahead, use your fingers to spread it around. Then generously sprinkle on the sugar. Bake. The top will be wonderfully crispy, and your guests will be so impressed with your wonderful culinary skills.

Serve this meal with a mixed green salad. I like to use the mixed wild greens you can get today, and I add a bunch of red or green grape halves or ripe diced pear. Toss with a honey mustard dressing. Finish it off with hot crusty rolls and you've got a meal fit for a queen. Or your very best friend. Whatever you do, enjoy. And serve with love.

Ida Mae Tutweiler

More New Releases from Authorlink Press

Magee's Blue #3 (Apr.00, $14.95, ISBN 1928704123) by Donald Whittington. *Mainstream fiction.* The touching story of a rural family determined to stick together against all odds, and of a young boy's struggle to deal with self-blame.

Twin City (Apr 00, $14.95, ISBN 1928704131) by Jerry Lee Davis. *Mainstream Fiction.* The son of rural, Baptist parents comes of age through his friendship with the daughter of the only Jewish family in a small Georgia town.

Pretty Is Just A Face I Make (Apr.00, $14.95, ISBN 192870414X) by Ellen Mae Smith. *Mainstream fiction.* Lynn works as a stripper to save for college, discovering the tenuous line between what she will and won't do for money and salvation. Based on true events.

By An Eldritch Sea (Apr.00, $14.95, ISBN 1928704166) by Carolee Joy. *Paranormal Romance.* A Romance Writers of America Golden Heart Finalist. Marine biologist Kelsey MacKenzie's scientific world collides with Scotland's legendary selkies when she meets Cade Douglas, who has a mysterious link to the enchanted race who are seals in the water and human on land. Cade wrestles with ancient tradition while desire irrevocably draws him to the daughter of his family's sworn enemy.

Books of Similar Interest From Authorlink Press

Snapshots (ISBN 1928704018), by Kimbra Martin a touching portrayal of the horrors of child sexual abuse, and the triumph of the human spirit. "*Snapshots is the voice for every woman ever abused as a child.*"—*Midwest Book Review.* Amazon Customer Reviewer rating: 5 stars

Five Keys for Understanding Men (ISBN 192870400X), by Gary L. Malone, MD and Susan Mary Malone. A male psychoanalyst shares his experiences to help women truly understand men's drives, needs and desires. Amazon.com customer reviewer rating: 5 Stars

Wild Angel (ISBN 1928704042), by Carolee Joy, a contemporary romance. Amazon.com reviewer rating: 5 stars

Madonna of the Dark (ISBN 1928704026), by Elaine Moore, a vampire novel. Ranked 4 1/2 stars. *"A brilliantly crafted, exceptionally well written novel that is as seminal a contribution to the vampire genre as are the novels of Anne Rice or Chelsea Quinn Yarbro." —Midwest Book Review, Oct, 1999.* Amazon.com reviewer rating: 4 1/2 stars

See all of our Authorlink Press titles at www.authorlink.com, or visit our secure electronic store at www.authorlink.net. Titles usually fast ship within 48 hours.

90000
9 781928 704157